The String Effect Vol One

This is a story about how love can turn into infatuation.

By Alfred K Watson

Acknowledgement & Dedication

I would like to give thanks to God for giving me the will, the insight and the desire to write this book.

I would like to dedicate this book to my parents Sylvia and Frank Watson. Without them, I wouldn't be the man that I am today. I also would like to give special thanks to all the women who taught me how to love and appreciate the value of a relationship. To my kids, I will love you always!

Table of Contents

Chapter One

The Search Begins

My story begins with a fine young man named Alvin. He has a pecan Complexion, a ripped body, and stands at a fierce 6'6" tall. Now with all his good looks, Alvin also actually has a great job as an IT manager at an excellent law firm. You would think that a brother this fine would have women all over the place. He grew up in a church environment, but really doesn't go as often as he should. He still keeps those good old wholesome values though. He still believes that one day he'll find the woman of his dreams and spend the rest of his life with her. That might sound good, but the reality is, love is tricky.

Young Alvin, who always wants to do the right thing, seems to fall short of his dreams and glories. Take Keisha for example, a slim, sexy, light-skinned diva. On his way to work one day, he ran into Keisha while going to the coffee shop. For him it was love at first sight. Like the gentleman that he is, he opened the door for her, and with a very sexy smile he said, "Good morning". She was so taken by his good looks and charm, she flashed back a big flirtatious smile with a twinkle in her eyes and said, "Thank you".

Alvin stood behind her in line as she placed her order. He stared, and made sure that he studied her body from the top of her head to the bottom of her toes.

Like a detective, he analyzed everything about her. Her hair was neat, and definitely not fake. She wore a nice brown business suit, highlighted with the perfect heels to show off her smooth sexy legs. He also took a whiff of her perfume, which seemed to put him into an immediate trance. Not being able to take it anymore, Alvin leaned over her shoulder and politely said, "I would be honored if you let me pay for your breakfast."

Keisha turned around and looked straight into his eyes, "First off, I don't even know who you are. Why would I let you do that?"

Alvin used the deepest pitch of his bass voice, "Well my name is Alvin, and because if you don't let me buy your breakfast, then I would never forgive myself for letting this opportunity slip by. You happen to be the most beautiful woman I have ever seen."

"I'm sure as fine as you are, you must have used that line on countless other women. I'm Keisha."

"Nice to meet you Keisha. I would however like you to know that I am very single, and extremely interested in getting to know you. I would love it if you take my business card and think about us having dinner within the very near future,"

Keisha reach for the card and then placed it into her purse. "You must be one of those smooth talking brothers that my mother warned me about. I Must say that you have my attention Mr. Alvin. I would take you up on that offer, and by the way, my tab is $5.69."

As Alvin told the cashier he would pay for her order, she took her bag and glided toward the door with such a sexy, seductive walk. She turned around just before reaching for the door and said, "Mr. Alvin,

I will call you later on tonight, I hope none of your lady friends or wife pick up when I call."

Alvin looked back and got a full view of Keisha and her body, "Don't worry, I will be the only one picking up my phone, and I will be waiting very eagerly for your call. Just don't have me waiting too long to hear your beautiful voice."

Alvin was smiling as if he won the lottery. All day long he had a big childish grin on his face of accomplishment.

Later on that night, Keisha called and Alvin was very excited that she even called at all. They talked about everything for hours, from about 9:00 p.m. to 5:45 a.m. in the morning. Just before they hung up, Keisha was starting to get a little bit personal asking about Alvin's sex life. She asked, "Why a good-looking brother at 32 years old with a great job, an excellent sense of humor and who could talk about everything and anything under the sun is still single."

Alvin chuckled to himself because he knew that question was coming, "Listen, I already know that I could go around and have as many women as I want. I am not about that life. I am looking to settle down with someone who is worthy of being my wife. Right now I really don't have time for all the games. I've actually had my fun when I was younger and now I am ready to commit my body, my soul, and my heart to that very special woman."

Alvin heard Keisha clapping her hands in the back ground. "Good answer! So what makes you think that I might be that right woman for you?"

There was a hush over the phone for a few seconds as if Alvin wasn't there. Then Alvin said, "I never said you were the right person for me, but I like everything that I heard about you so far. I just hoped that we could get to know one another and take it from there."

Keisha was very impress with all of Alvin answers, but wanted to dig more. "Okay I can understand that, but I have to be honest with you; I definitely need a man that knows how to throw down in the bedroom because I tend to get bored very quickly."

Alvin did not hesitate and replied with confidents, "I assure you, when it comes to the bedroom; I am one who will always fulfill all of your needs and desires."

Keisha started laughing hysterically, "If I had a dollar from every man who has told me that, I would be the richest women in the world right now!"

Alvin whose ego was bruised by her comments was the type of man that, if you were to throw out a challenge, he would be more than happy to take it. "Well you do know there is only one way to find that out right? Unfortunately, I would truly prefer to get to know you a whole lot better before I am able to prove to you how much of a great lover I am."

Keisha sighed with disappointment, "So let me get this straight, you want me to be all emotionally attached to you before I can find out if you're as good as you claim you are in the bedroom? Listen baby, just like you at the age of twenty-nine, I am not getting any younger. I can honestly admit that it would be nice to settle down, but I'm sorry; To me the love making thing have to be on point. I'm employed, I have my own place, and I can take care of myself. I don't really need or want a man for his money. The only real requirement that I have for my man, is to have what it takes to make me go to sleep after some good, hot, sexy love making, then there is no need for me to be looking any further."

After listening to everything that Keisha said, he started smiling to himself because he remembers how beautiful and sexy she looks. "Okay; This would go against everything that I believe in, but I'll tell you what. How about this weekend you come over to my place? I'll cook you a nice dinner and after that we can dance to some good old fashioned old school slow jams. Afterwards if the vibes are there, then we can come to my bedroom and make some sweet love all night long. Now depending on how well you approve of my love making skills, and if you were to stick around, I will make sure to serve you breakfast in bed in the morning."

Keisha told Alvin to hold on while she walks to her bedroom and lay down. Once she was comfortable, in a very sexy soft voice she said, "I don't want you to think that I am that kind of lady that would just jump into bed with someone that I barely know. After talking to you tonight, I feel as though as that I could be very honest with you without feeling ashamed. Everything that you just said to me fucking turned me on. I'm like literally very wet and horny just thinking about all of that. I don't know if it's the tone of your deep voice or what, but no man has ever made me feel this way just by talking to him over the phone."

Alvin softly started pounding his chest so that Keisha couldn't hear him. "Well I am glad that you were able to be honest with me. I don't want you to think that I am that type of guy either to just jump in the bed like that. I really do like you and hope that when you come over, it would be something that we both can look back on and remember forever.

So listen, we've been up all night talking and I can't believe that it's actually time for me to get ready for work. Before I let you go though, there is one thing that I want you to know and keep in your mind as you start your day. When it comes to wetness, I have the right experience and tools to dry everything all up."

Keisha took a deep breath and moaned out, "Stop that! You keep talking to me like that I am going to make you talk dirty to me. Then you really would be late for work!"

They both said their goodbyes and hung up. During that whole week, Keisha and Alvin continued to have interesting and steamy conversations at night until the wee hours of the morning. When the weekend came around, Alvin made sure that everything was just right at his place. He brought some scented candles home and placed them all around in order to give each room just the right amount of light. He made a nice pan of four-cheese lasagna from scratch. He also went out and purchased some Champaign and a dozens of red and white roses. Alvin was very excited about the atmosphere he had created, and he knew that Keisha was going to be pleased.

When Keisha arrived, she rung the bell and Alvin went to greet her at the door with the roses in his hands. When Alvin opened up the door, he became numb as soon as he saw how she looked. Keisha arrived late but he could see why. She was looking like a sexy high-class diva with just the right amount of lady-of-the-night seduction.

She wore a nice, low cut black blouse that showed the top of her breasts with lace patterns, and a black leather mini skirt that just barely covered her butt. She had on a black pair of fishnet stockings and a pair of five-inch black leather high heel shoes. She wore her hair down and straightened, just barely touching her shoulders. Her nails were manicured with a fire-red color and her lips were glossed with red of the same shade. She was wearing the same perfume that she had worn when he first met her, but the fragrance was just a little bit stronger.

Alvin was not only pleased with how Keisha was looking, but in his mind he knew he was going to bang the hell out of her when that time came. Alvin took Keisha's coat and gave her the roses. "When I saw these at the flower shop, I fell in love with them as soon as I saw them. I just knew I had to get them for you, because that was the same way I felt about you when I first saw you." Alvin said as he blushed.

Keisha gave Alvin a big hug. She held him tightly for a moment and then gave a kiss on the cheeks. "Aww it's been so long since someone bought me flowers. They are so beautiful, thank you Alvin."

Alvin didn't want to let her go. He leaned over again and gave a soft kiss on the lips and whispered, "Your welcome. It's already kind of late, so would you like to just go for dinner now and then we could relax a little bit later?"

Keisha looked a little embarrassed. "Well I guess I could eat now, I'm sorry that I'm a little late."

Alvin reassured her, "No; don't worry about that. I'm just glad to have you here.

Alvin lead her into his dining room.

"I hope you like Italian food. I've cooked my famous four cheese lasagna."

"Wow that sounds very good. I can't wait to taste it."

Being the perfect gentleman, Alvin did everything right that night. He served Keisha as if she was dining in a five-star restaurant. They talked and laughed, enjoying every bit of each other's company. When dinner was over Keisha offered to help Alvin with the dishes, but he politely declines. "Keisha, my beautiful sexy princess; Tonight everything that I do for you right here right now, I want to do with you for the rest of our lives."

Keisha started panting and fanning her face with her hands, "Wow, I never knew a man like you actually existed. All my life I have been meeting and dating losers. Sometimes a woman gets tired of the same old bull shit that men like to throw at us."

Alvin softly took her hands and looked deep into her eyes, "You should look at it this way; If it wasn't for all the BS that you went through, then how would you be able to really appreciate the real deal when it finally comes your way?"

Keisha stared passionately back at Alvin "You're right Alvin, if it wasn't for them, I wouldn't be here enjoying you. You and that nice sexy tight butt of yours. Did any woman ever tell you that you have such a nice sexy tight butt?"

Alvin began to blush, "No, but you know what they say. There's always a first time for everything."

Keisha reached around and softly caressed Alvin's butt. Then she thanked him for dinner. He brought her in front of his CD collection and told her to pick out something nice that she would like to hear while he placed the dishes in the dish washer. After washing the dishes, Alvin put on most of the songs that Keisha liked and a few of his own favorite nice, soft, old school slow jams.

They must have danced for about an hour before Alvin finally gazed into Keisha's eyes and started kissing her passionately. Keisha showed no resistance and just held him tighter and kissed him back while pressing her body firmly against his. Alvin grabbed Keisha's hands and led her into the bedroom. Alvin slowly started to remove Keisha clothes. When he was done, he laid her on the bed and took off his shirt. Keisha eyes lit up when she saw that Alvin was all muscles. She quickly raised up and removed his pants. Alvin was already erect and he forced her back down and started to passionately tongue kissing her. As he works his way down to her neck, Keisha body started to shake. Alvin felt her hot cum gushing on his legs and he went to investigate with his tongue. Again Keisha body started shaking, this time she grabs his head and yelled "I can't believe your fucking making me cum like this." Alvin reached for a condom and place it on his cock. As soon as he penetrated her, she started climaxing again.

Alvin made love to Keisha as if it was their last days on earth. They went at it all night long doing every position one could think of. As the sunlight shined into Alvin's bedroom window, Keisha laying on top of Alvin's chest said, "I have to admit, I've been with quite a few guys in my lifetime, but no one has ever made love to me like that before. You are totally awesome in everything that you do Alvin. I truly hope that I can live up to your expectations, because this is what I've been looking for."

Alvin, was so exhausted he couldn't even open up his eyes, "From the first time that I laid eyes on you, you met most if not all of my expectation without even saying one word. Giving me a chance and letting me get to know you was more like the icing on top of an already exceptional piece of cake."

Chapter Two

The Betrayal

They both fell asleep in each other's arms and enjoyed the rest of the weekend in bed making love.

Months went by, and it appeared that Alvin and Keisha had the perfect relationship. She spent a lot of time at his place and they even took weekend getaway trips just about every other weekend. All was going very well into their relationship until one morning at about 3:00 a.m., Keisha called Alvin sobbing on the phone.

Keisha, crying hysterically, said, "I'm sorry baby I didn't mean to hurt you; I didn't mean to hurt you."

"Baby what's going on? Why are you crying?"

Keisha sounding pathetic and increasingly desperate, "I want to tell you, but I really don't want to lose you."

"Come on babe it's too early in the morning for the games. Just tell me what's going on."

Keisha, started crying even harder and babbling her words, "My ex-boyfriend just left here and I did something really stupid and bad."

Alvin remained silent, waiting for Keisha to finish.

"My ex broke my ankle bracelet way before we met and he put it in the shop to get it fixed right before we broke up. He called me earlier in the day and said he got it fixed and wanted me to have it. I kept telling him that I didn't want it anymore, but he kept being so persistent about it. So I just told him to bring it over. When he came over I told him to just give it to me and leave, but it was like he wouldn't go unless he said what he had to say. I felt as though I didn't have a choice and as we talked about our past, somewhere in there I just got caught up and allowed my emotions to take over."

Alvin finally broke his silence. "So let me guess, you slept with him?"

Keisha kept quiet for a few seconds and then said, "Yes baby. I'm sorry, and now I am feeling so dirty. I really didn't want to hurt you or us baby, honest. Please understand that I am truly sorry and it will never ever happen again, I promise you that Alvin. I just want your forgiveness and I hope that we can still be together."

Again, Alvin kept quiet for a few seconds and then he spoke in a soft but hurt voice, "All this time we were spending together, how could you go and do something so stupid like that?"

Keisha replied, "I'm sorry baby but when I met you I have to admit, I still had feelings for him. When you came along you helped me get over him. I was trying to break up with him for years because I knew he wasn't any good for me. I don't know what I was thinking when I gave myself to him, but when it was all over, I was so upset with myself. I told him he had to leave and he left. That is when I called you.

"Alvin, I really didn't want to keep this a secret from you, just to show you how much I regret it and how much I love you. I realize that we have such a good thing going and I went ahead and messed it all up. I really need you to forgive me right now baby. I am hurting badly and I'm so in love with you."

Again Alvin kept silent, this time he took even longer to speak. But before he could say anything, Keisha, still sobbing said, "Alvin, are you still there? Please talk to me baby I need you to understand how much I love you and want to be with you."

Alvin sat up in his bed with the phone still pressed to his ears and said, "I am truly disappointed in you Keisha. I gave you one hundred percent of my wellbeing. I've treated you like the only person that ever mattered to me. How could you go out of your way and do this to me?"

Through the sobs, Keisha started repeating the word "please" over and over again. Alvin continued, "Keisha you know better than me that it's all about the trust, that's something I thought we truly never had to worry about. Not only did you betray me, but you broke whatever trust we built together. I am so beyond disappointed in you right now Keisha. As matter of fact, as of right now, this relationship is over. Please don't bother calling me anymore."

Alvin hung up the phone, but Keisha wasted no time calling him right back. Alvin answered the phone and in a thunderous voice said, "What?"

"Please Alvin, just give me one more chance. I promise that it will never happen again. I love you baby. Please give me another chance."

"Listen it's obvious that this will not be the last time, because I remember you telling me that you love a man that knows how to throw down in the bedroom. So if he was hitting it like that, then I'm sorry, I don't think you will ever be able to let him go. He is going to always find a way to try and see you. I call it the string effect. Either you are stringing him along, just to keep him in your life, or he's doing that to you. Either way I don't want any parts of it. So if you don't mind, I have to get up in a few hours and I need to get some sleep."

Alvin hung up the phone once again. This time Keisha didn't call back. A few weeks went by and even though Keisha called a few times and left messages for Alvin, they never spoke. Alvin although on the outside seemed to be okay with not talking to Keisha, he was really hurting on the inside because he knew that deep down he was really in love in her. There were many nights that he would just lay there in his bed and think about calling her to try and patch things up, but in the end he decided that she really wasn't healthy for him. So he resisted temptation long enough so as time went by, he was able to suppress any thoughts of seeing her.

Chapter Three

New Love Emerges

A couple more months went by and Keisha was totally out of Alvin's system. One day when all of his staff was out to lunch, Alvin received an urgent phone call to fix a computer that was down in the law office. Since none of his staff was in the office, he decided to take the call himself. When he reached the main floor his boss asked him to work his magic on a computer that had to be repaired and updated to run on the company's LAN network. He informed Alvin that he had a new associate working for him and she wanted to use her own laptop, but it seemed to be plagued with viruses so it had to be fixed before hooking it up to the main frame.

"No problem, of course", Alvin replied. Alvin started walking with his boss Mr. Charles and they both walked up to meet Ms. Monica Jackson at her desk. Alvin's jaws seemed to dropped to the ground when he laid eyes on her. Monica was a very sexy dark skinned chocolate diva. Although she was big boned, when she stood up to shake Alvin's hands, he immediately noticed the hourglass curves that she possessed. Like before, Alvin instantaneously sized her up. The gray dress that she was wearing looked like it had been poured onto her body, hitting every curve perfectly.

Her breasts were kind of big, but he could tell that they could stand up on their own without a bra. Her hair was dark brown with a slight tint of blond that fell to the small of her back. Although he very much liked her hair, this time he knew that it wasn't all hers. Her face was even perfect without the help of any makeup. She only had a slight touch of lip-gloss on to highlight her juicy small lips. Her nails were well done and a little long, but they were her own nails. Her legs were thick, but they complimented every other part of her body. *She really knows how to wear those heels* he thought to himself.

His boss, Mr. Charles introduce them and told Alvin, "I know it's going to be a little hard fixing her computer, but try your best to concentrate on the computer and not her." Both Alvin and Monica laughed.

Alvin looked at Mr. Charles with a big grin on his face. "Mr. Charles, I am going to try my best, but you sure know how to put pressure on a brother."

"Well I'm glad that you were the one to come down, because you are not only our best IT tech, but your professionalism always speaks volumes to me," said Mr. Charles, giving a wink at Alvin.

"Okay Mr. Charles, please tell me how much it's going to cost me for you tell Ms. Monica all of that nice stuff about me?"

Mr. Charles laughed and said, "I was just laying down the ground work, the rest is up to you. Besides, I meant every word that I've said."
Mr. Charles winked at Monica and left. Monica sat back down at her desk and Alvin pulled up a chair and started working on her laptop.

"So you're the famous Alvin that all of the women around here have been talking about?"

"What are you talking about?" Alvin replied, blushing slightly.

"I was warned that the sexiest guy in the office was the IT manager."

Alvin couldn't help it and stopped working on Monica's laptop just to look into her eyes. "So that's the rumor that is going on around here, huh?"

Starring back him, Monica, in a sexy soft voice said, "Hmm I really can't say that it's a rumor now that I am seeing you in person for myself."

Alvin started back working, and tried not to look back at her. "Well if there is any consolation, I happen to think that you are definitely the sexiest lawyer in the entire country. Maybe even the whole wide world!"

Monica placed both her hands under her chin and said, "Oh really now? Hmm, I don't know, but maybe I need to keep my computer down so that I could have you come to my rescue all the time."

Again Alvin looked up into Monica's big beautiful hazel eyes, "I really don't like to work too hard on the job, so if you really want to see me, all you have to do is take my card and call me any time after hours."

Monica leaned back and flirtatiously licked her lips, "Wow the new girl on the block getting the number? I was told that there wasn't a chance in hell that you would be seen with anyone around here in the office."

"Well you are very right about that; I don't like mixing business with pleasure. To be honest, I don't really know why I just did that. You must be one hell of a lawyer."

"Why would you say that?" Monica replied with a smirk.

"Because in just a short time after meeting you and being in your presence, I was already convinced by your skills to do exactly what you wanted me to do. If I was sitting as a jury on your one of your cases, you would have already had me in your pockets."

Monica laughed showing her beautiful white teeth, "You're crazy; I didn't make you to do anything that you already had in your mind of doing."

"Okay you got me there, I must admit that from the moment that I laid eyes on you, I felt an urge to know a little more about you." Alvin finished running a few programs on Monica's computer and told her that she was all set. "Thank you Mr. Alvin. And now that I have your card, when would be the best time to use it?"

"Well, whenever you need me to fix your computer at work, you can call me anytime. But if you ever want to see me after hours, then again, I would suggest that you call me anytime. I am here to serve you twenty-four hours a day, seven days a week."

Again Monica licked her lips and said in a soft, sexy voice "Yes, I like that. I am going to give you a call later on tonight. Let me find out that I have my very own twenty-four hours' maintenance man."

Alvin packed up his tools and placed both his hands on Monica's desk, "I don't know all about that maintenance man stuff, but yes, you do have access to a reliable brother when you need one."

Later on that night, Monica called Alvin and told him that he was on her mind all day. Since Alvin was such a smooth talker, they talked all night long into the wee hours of the morning. The best thing Alvin could have found out about Monica is the fact that she got married when she was young and it didn't work out. Her Husband had left her for another woman and it has scorned her very badly. She tried, but never had any kids with him, and both of her parents were deceased. She also was an only child who lived with her aunt most of her life until she passed away just a couple of years ago. Basically, Monica was in every since of the word, a true *strong black woman* who had overcome a rough childhood and made something of herself. She would have made her parents proud.

The next day while at the office, Monica called Alvin and asked if he would have lunch with her. Alvin, who was in his office with Joseph, a member of his crew, said, "I am really short on staff today and don't even think that I will be able to take lunch at all today".

Monica, sounding disappointed, said, "Aw poor baby, would you like for me to bring you something back since you are too busy to go out?"

"Wow, if I didn't know any better, I'd think you were trying to soften me up for the kill."

Monica was shocked when she heard Alvin's response, "Excuse me! Listen, I admit that I like you a lot, especially after our conversation last night; But don't let it get to your head. I was fine before I met you, and I will be fine after knowing you."

Alvin appeared to be a little confused, "Listen, I was only joking when I said that. I actually accept your offer if you still have it on the table."

"Yes the offer is still available and I am sorry for going off like that. Sometimes I get a little peeved when someone takes my kindness for some kind of motive."

"I apologize for that. I can understand where you are coming from."

"Good, then we are on the same page. So what would you like for me to bring you?"

"I'm really not hungry but I will take a chicken salad with some French dressing."

"Okay, I know this great spot that I went to the other day. They make great salads there. I will bring it to your office when I get back."

Alvin agreed and said, "Thank you."

After they hung up, Joseph who was listening to their conversation turned to Alvin and said, "I heard you bagged the new chick in the Law office. Go ahead player with your bad self. I saw her the other day and almost fell of the cliff. They need to put a sign near her desk that says, "Caution Dangerous Curves ahead!"

Alvin started laughing, "Joe you're crazy, I haven't bagged anything. We are just talking for now, nothing more. So stop spreading the rumors like everybody else around here."

"So does that mean I can go for mine? You know there is a lot of things I could do with a nice honey like that."

"Hell no! I might be stupid, but I am not a fool. Don't worry I'm working on it. What you really need to do is finish up on all of this work we have around here and let me worry about the ladies while you worry about keeping your job!"

"That's cold man, but okay you're right. I do have a lot to do, but the next fine honey that comes to work here is mine."

Alvin continued working until Monica called and said that she was coming up. When she arrived, they both sat down and had their lunch in his office, and talked about going to see a Broadway play. Monica said, "You know I've been in the city for years and never went to see a play on Broadway."

"Really! Girl you just don't know what you have been missing. It would be an honor to be the first person to take you to see a play."

Monica with a great big smile on her face said, "Umm, I think I am really going to like spending time with you." She leaned over and gave him a soft kiss on the cheek. "Listen babe I have to get back to work, but I will give you a call later on tonight to see when we are going to make all of this happen.

"Well I do like the babe part. I definitely wouldn't mind being your babe."

"Don't let that go to your head, I just about call everyone babe. It's just a bad habit that I have," Monica said.

Alvin looked a little disappointed, "Okay I can understand that. Call me later on tonight and we will discuss the details after I do some research on a nice one to go and see."

Monica agreed and she left his office. The look on Alvin's face was priceless as he watched Monica leave his office.

Later on that night, Monica called Alvin and he thanked her for coming to his office and having lunch with him. He also started pouring out about how he was starting to get feelings for her.

"Listen, I just got out of a relationship in which I thought it was going somewhere and I ended up getting a little hurt., I have to be honest with you; I actually thought it would take a while before I found someone that I wanted to be with again."

Monica cooed, "Aw poor baby got his feelings hurt, tell mommy what happened."

Alvin proceeded to tell Monica what happened between him and Keisha. When he was finished, he added that he really developed deep feelings for Keisha and that he has a love for her that has slowly gone away.

"Wow, I am sorry you had to go through that. You don't have to worry about any of my ex's coming back into this picture. I haven't been in a relationship in seven years. After my divorce, I've been busy trying to get my degrees and making things happen in my life. I am pretty much content on who I am and where I want to be."

"The moment I started talking to you, I knew you had your shit together. I think that was one of the things I liked most about you. Not to mention the fact that you have that banging body," Alvin said as he laughed.

"Oh please you know it was all about the booty when you first saw me stop fronting," Monica quipped.

"Yes you do have a very nice behind if I must say so myself. Are you going to let me hit that?"

"What! No you did not just ask me that question."

Alvin quickly said, "I was only playing; you know I want more than that from you."

"You wasn't playing, but I will tell you what, when the time is right you are going to know it."

Alvin replied "When the time is right for that to happen, then you will know how serious I am about you."

"I will keep that in mind Mr. sexy man,"

Alvin told Monica that he already purchased the tickets for this weekend to see a play. They were both excited and talked about it a little more before they hung up and went to sleep. The next day at work, Joseph asked Alvin, "What is going on between you and Miss Monica? Man, that chick is fine as hell!"

Alvin replied, "I like her a lot. I'm actually going to take her to see this play on the weekend."

"Wow you are the man. By the way, after you left yesterday, Keisha called and said to tell you that she was still thinking about you. She wanted you to call her. What's up with that?"

"Damn, I thought she would have moved on by now. That chick is someone who you wouldn't mind on your arm, but in the end you know she is going to be bad for you. Right now I am not trying to be hear her man, I just want to put all of my concentration on Monica and be happy."

"I hear you man, Monica really seems like a wonderful woman. I want you to know that I am pulling for you."

Alvin thanked Joseph for the message and told him to get back to work. Later that day, Alvin wanted to surprise Monica with lunch, but he found out that she would be tied up in court all day. That night he called Monica and they talked about each other's day. Monica was so excited about going to see the play tomorrow, that they didn't want stay on the phone too long. She told Alvin that she had a very long exhausting day. Alvin agreed and said, "Goodnight baby, you know I am going to be dreaming about you all night."

Monica kissed the phone so that Alvin could have heard it. "You are going to be in my dreams as well sexy, goodnight."

Early that morning while Alvin was looking for something to wear for the show, the doorbell rang. Alvin went to the door and saw that it was Keisha. He cracked the door open and looked at her with disgust, "What are you doing here?"

"I've tried calling you and leaving you messages but you never called me back, so I just came over because I wanted to talk to you."

In a nasty tone Alvin said, "Listen, we really don't have anything to talk about, what we had is over."

Keisha's eyes started to tear up and her face became flushed, "I messed up Alvin I know that, but why can't you at least find it in your heart just to be a friend to me. I really miss talking to you, and sometimes I just want someone to tell me that everything is going to be alright. I didn't mean to hurt you Alvin, and if I could find a way to take it all back I would. Besides that, I really wish that you would let me in so that we could have this conversation in the house. I really hate talking to you through this little opening in the door."

Alvin hesitated and then opened the door to let Keisha in. Keisha without asking went and sat on the sofa and continued talking. "Alvin, look at me. I am going to admit that I am always going to be in love with you. It pains me to know that I can't hold you and kiss you anymore. It pains me to know that we are not talking to each other anymore. It's been months now and I just want this pain to stop hurting."

Keisha started crying and Alvin walked over to her and handed her a tissue. "Keisha listen, you weren't the only one hurting. I fell in love with you too and you completely shattered my heart with what you had done. How am I ever going to trust you again? I actually thought that we were perfect for each other in every way. You know even now when I look at you, I can only think about the fact that someone else had you in a way that was supposed to be something special, just for me. Okay if you want a friend, I can be a friend. But that is all I will be to you. I've actually moved on and I am happy where I am right now."

Keisha stopped sobbing and looked Alvin deeply into his eyes, "So what do you mean? Are you already seeing someone else?"

"Yes, I started seeing someone else and I'm really into her right now. I had to learn to move on with my feelings for you."

Keisha put her arms around Alvin waist and said, "Look me in the eyes and tell me that you still don't love me."

Alvin wasn't able to look at Keisha, but pulled away from her, "I may be still in love with you, but I just happen to love myself even more. Besides, the real reality of it all is the fact that, if you truly loved me the way you said that you do, then we wouldn't be at this point in the first place."

Keisha became angry and stood in front of Alvin and started shouting in his face. "You act like you're Mr. Perfect. Like you never did anything wrong in your life to ask for forgiveness. All I was asking was for you to forgive me and give me another chance. I didn't have to call you that night! You wouldn't even know anything unless I told you."

"I cared enough about you to be honest with you. I poured out my heart, hurting with every word, letting you know that I have made a huge mistake and you repay me by breaking up with me. I needed you that night Alvin. I wanted you to understand that I never ever wanted another man to touch me again besides you. I felt that way that night, and I feel that way now."

Tears started rolling down Alvin's face. He looked down at her and pushed his middle finger on her forehead, "I know how you felt, but you have no Idea how you made me feel. I told you from day one that I wanted a woman that I could call my own. I told you that I wanted to be with you for the rest of my life. Didn't my words mean anything to you? How could I give you one hundred percent of my being and essence, when you turn around and gave me fifty percent?"

Getting louder Alvin continued, "How can I love a woman who cannot stop herself from having sex with another man who really doesn't give a damn about her? How do you expect me to be able to call you my wife, when you didn't even respect me as your man? I'm sorry, but after thinking about all of that, I couldn't even be your friend. I think you need to leave!"

Keisha was speechless, but she understood everything that Alvin just said. She walked toward the door and turned around, she then grabbed Alvin by the hands, "Just because I understand what you are saying right now doesn't take away from how I feel about you." As she tried to reach up and give him a kiss on the lips, Alvin slightly turned his head and she caught him on the cheeks.

"I will always love you, Alvin," Keisha turned around and then walked out the door.

Alvin was a little shaken, but he knew he had to get ready for his date with Monica tonight. As night fell, Monica and Alvin met up and had a great time at the show. Alvin took Monica home and stood with her at the front of her door.

Monica stared at Alvin and placed her arms around him. "Wow, I really had a lovely time with you tonight Alvin. I actually wish that this night didn't have to end."

Alvin placed his forehead on top of hers and looked into her eyes. He then gave her a very passionate, wet tongue kiss. "I don't want the night to end either, but I do want to respect you, not only today, but if possible for the rest of my life." He then explained to her that there would be plenty of nights like this and that there was no need to rush into anything.

Monica smiled and started kissing Alvin again, "Oh, you turning down booty? That's a first for me."

Alvin looked at Monica cautiously because he didn't know if she was being serious or just messing with him. "Now we both agreed we would know when the time was right. As much as I would like to come inside and be with you, I don't think we should go there tonight."

Monica released her arms from around Alvin and softly pushed him away. "I understand where you are coming from Alvin. Just as long as you are going to respect me, I am always going to respect you."

He gave her another Passionate kiss and went to his car. Many weeks went by and the relationship between Monica and Alvin grew stronger. Both Monica and Alvin were saying to each other that they were the best thing that ever happened in each other's lives. The more time that they spent together, the stronger their relationship grew.

One Sunday evening, Keisha called Alvin and asked if he can come over and look at her desk top Computer. She told him that the guys from the geek squad came over, but they wanted to charge her an arm and a leg to get it fixed. Alvin started out being very sarcastic, "Please, do you really think I want to come over to your place and fix your computer? Nice try, but perhaps you need to find yourself someone else."

"Okay it's been awhile since we talked. I know that you are seeing someone else and I am not trying to trick you into anything." Keisha said. "All I want you to do is come over and to see if you can fix my computer. I want nothing more, nothing less."

Chapter Four

A New String Forms

Alvin was getting some very strong negative bad vibes from Keisha, so he stuck to his guns.

"Alvin, I know you didn't want to be my friend, but I really need my computer fixed. I don't have the hundreds of dollars to get it fixed, but I am willing to give you some money if you can do this for me."

Alvin finally broke down and agreed. He told Keisha that he would be there within an hour. When Alvin arrived, Keisha opened the door and Alvin saw that Keisha wasn't wearing anything sexy. He never remembered seeing her so plain and down-to-earth. Keisha invited him in and said, "I would give you a kiss, but I'm not trying to scare you. I really just want you to take a look at my computer and tell me if you can fix it."

"Yes, a kiss would definitely be a deal breaker and scare me. But let me tell you something. After all this time that has gone by, this is me trying to make an attempt at being your friend. I do not want anything from you, and I'm damn sure don't want to talk about our past or about us being together."

Keisha nodded her head in agreement. An hour has passed, and while Alvin was working on her computer, he happened to look up at Keisha while she wasn't looking. In his mind he said, "Damn, after not seeing her for all this time, I forgot how beautiful she is." However, that thought left as quickly as it had entered his mind.

It took about two hours for Alvin to actually fix Keisha's computer. During that whole time, she didn't say a word except to offer him something to drink or eat.

"Here you go, it's good as new."

"Thank you Alvin, if it's okay I would love to give you a hug because you don't know how much I really needed my computer."

Alvin hesitated and said, "I guess I could give you a hug." He gave her a very friendly hug and a peck on the cheeks, and told her that he had to go.

Keisha walked him to the door and said, "Thank you again Alvin, I promise not to call you anymore for anything. But if you like, you can call me anytime, even if it's to talk about nothing."

"I will do that. And for the record Keisha, I forgive you."

Alvin left, but if he had turned around when he walked away, he would have seen a single tear dripping down Keisha's face, along with a smile of vindication.

When Alvin reached home he checked his messages and saw that Monica was trying to reach him. She left a message saying that she was in a car accident with her friends. She was okay, but one of her friends was banged up pretty bad and was in the hospital. She asked if he could give her a call as soon as he got the message. She also wanted to know if he could pick her up from the hospital. Alvin called her and then went to meet her at the hospital. He was so happy to see that she was alright.

Both Monica and Alvin stood holding each other in the waiting room. Alvin gazed into Monica eyes and said, "Baby I was so scared when I heard your messages. Under no circumstance do I want anything to happen to you. I feel as though you are a part of me now, and just like my fingers, my arms and my feet, I never want to live without you."

Monica smiled and said, "You are a one of a kind man Alvin, and to my very last breath I will always love you. You complete me!" They held each other for a few moments and Monica decided that she wanted to spend the night over at Alvin's place because she was too shaken up to stay at home alone.

After reaching Alvin's home they both agreed to take the next day off. While they laid in the bed, Monica turned to Alvin and said, "Babe, where were you all day when I was trying to reach you?"

Alvin was surprised by the question, he took a deep breath and said, "Listen baby, I know this is going to sound really crazy right now, but I can't lie to you. Out of respect I am going to tell you the truth. I was at Keisha's house working on her computer. She told me that she couldn't afford to get it fixed and I guess I felt a little sorry for her and fixed it for nothing."

Monica rolled over and stared at the blank walls. Alvin tried to put his arms around her but she quickly pushed them off. Alvin took another deep breath, "I promise you that absolutely nothing happened between us. I fixed her computer, and I left."

Monica turned around, but there were a few tears in her eyes. She looked at Alvin in his face and said, "Since you feel like telling the truth, did you at any time kiss her?"

Alvin thought about it and said in a squeaking low voice, "Damn, I gave her a peck on the cheeks when I was leaving. But baby listen, like I said, it's not what you think."

Monica got off the bed and started putting on her clothes. Alvin tried to stop her but she shoved him hard onto the bed. She looked at Alvin and said, "While I could have lost my life tonight, you were playing *Mr. Fix It* at your ex's house. How do you think that makes me feel Alvin?"

Alvin stood up again, this time not touching Monica, "Damn babe, the entire time that I was there I not only respected you, but I respected us as a couple."

Monica complexion turned darker and she quickly slapped Alvin in the face. "If you really respected me, if you really respected us, you wouldn't have gone over there in the first place. Not to mention kissing her!"

Alvin still feeling the sting from the slap yelled out, "Fuck! You did not have to hit me. What in the hell is wrong with you? Now listen, if there is one thing that you need to know it's this. I really do love you, probably more than I love myself. Now God knows how much I love myself, but I am truly in love with you Monica. When I told you earlier that you are a part of me, I really do mean that shit."

Monica sarcastically started laughing, "If I knew you were with that bitch earlier, I would have never said the things I said to you in that damn hospital."

"I know you are upset right now and that's rightfully so. I know I messed up, although it's not as bad as you're making it out to be right now. Keisha means absolutely nothing to me. I hope you are not going to let something as small as this get in the way of what could be a very beautiful relationship?"

Monica held up one finger and started shaking her head and body, "See that's the problem. To you it may look like a little thing, but to me it's one of the worst things you could have ever done to us."

Monica finished getting dressed and Alvin told her to wait there. He went into the living room and came back. He got down on one knee and pulled out a stunning diamond engagement ring.

Alvin said, "I was trying to find the right time to give you this, but before you walk out of that door, I want you to know that I love you with all of my heart. I'm begging you, please don't make this misunderstanding get in the way of our future. Would you please marry me?"

Monica had a very hurtful, and sad look on her face, "I'm glad that you thought about me enough to be your wife, but today, right here, right now, is definitely not the right time. To me it seems as though you are taking how I feel and this situation lightly. Like I told you before, I could have lost my life tonight. Because of that, I'm actually hurt by you Alvin. I need some time to think about whether or not this is what I truly want. I'm sorry, but I can't accept your ring."

Monica told Alvin that she was going to take the bus or cab home. Alvin offered many times to drive her home, but each time she refused. Before Monica left, Alvin asked her to at least call or text him to let him know that she arrived home safely. Monica Agreed and she left.

Alvin was up all night. All he could think about was how messed up things were between him and Monica. An hour later, Monica texted Alvin letting him know that she made it home okay. A little later that night, he tried calling Monica, but she refused to answer the phone. Alvin didn't want to leave a message because he knew how annoying it was when he was receiving messages from Keisha. That whole night he just laid in the bed thinking about what he could have done differently.

The next morning, he decided to call Keisha. When Keisha answered the phone, Alvin said, "Damn Keisha, you really messed me up yesterday."

"Alvin, what are you taking about? I didn't do anything to you."

"I know, but if I didn't come to your house yesterday, I wouldn't be having problems in my relationship right now."

"We didn't do anything Alvin and you know that. I do appreciate you fixing my computer, but I honestly didn't want you to get into any trouble. That's exactly the reason why I dressed down when you came over. I didn't want you to think that I was trying to do anything. Although my feelings run very deep for you Alvin, I'm always going to love you forever. So if you are happy with your new love, then I am actually very happy for you."

"I know that, but I did violate my trust with her by coming over to your house without letting her know."

Keisha chuckled and said, "What is with you and this trust thing? If you recall, I was pretty much in your shoes a few months ago. I don't mean to add salt to your injuries, but now you know how much it sucks to be me!"

Alvin started laughing at Keisha's comments, "Okay Keisha, I understand how you feel now, but you have to understand that you slept with your ex. That was a pure violation of trust. All I did was come over and fix your damn computer. If you ask me that's comparing apples with oranges."

"Yes you are right Alvin. I'm sorry for making that statement. I'm just glad that you could call me and tell me about your problems. It really makes me happy that you could do that. Perhaps maybe now if things don't work out with you and her, you could give me another chance?"

"Keisha, deep down in my bones I do still love you, but I am very much in love with Monica. I ask her to be my wife and she turned me down. I will definitely try again in the near future. If or when I'm satisfied that it's never going to happen with her, then maybe I will consider your request."

Keisha was very disappointed with what Alvin just told her, "You proposed to her? At least she got further than I did. Alvin, I am going to show you not only how much I love you, but I'm also going to show you how much I will value our friendship."

Keisha asked Alvin for Monica's phone number so that she could tell her what really happened that day with the hope of repairing their relationship. Alvin thought about it for a few seconds, "There is no way in hell am I going to give my ex-girlfriend my present woman's phone number. Like really, what have you been smoking?"

"Damn Alvin, I only have your best interest at heart. Let me fix this for you, I owe you one."

Alvin was quiet for a moment and then said, "No; I'm not going to do that, but I really appreciate the fact that you wanted to help me out. Thanks Keisha."

"No problem. I just want you to know that I am here for you. As much as I would like to be with you, your happiness will always be my top priority."

"Well I really do appreciate your friendship now more than anything else," Alvin said. "I am going to hang up and give her another call. Hopefully she will answer the phone this time."

They both hung up the phone and Alvin tried calling Monica, but again he just reached her answering machine. The next day while Alvin was at work, he tried his best to stay in his office as he didn't want to run into Monica without knowing how she felt about him. He also grew jumpy each time the phone rang, hoping that it was her calling. Toward the end of the day when he didn't hear from her, he decided to go to her office to see how she was doing. On his way there he ran into his boss Mr. Charles.

"Woo there, I hope you are not planning to go see Monica?"

"Actually that is exactly where I'm going."

"Listen, let me save you the trouble. This morning she came to me and asked for a transfer. Now I don't know what happened between you two, but she has become one of my best lawyers. I had to jump through hoops just to get her here and I'm not trying to lose her over some office romance. So as your boss, I'm going to have to ask that you leave her alone and give it some time to cool off."

Looking both shocked and heartbroken, Alvin agreed not to speak to her on company time. Later that night Monica gave Alvin a call. Although Alvin was happy that she was calling, he answered the phone with a very uncaring "Hello."

Monica said, "I was surprised not to see you at work today.

"Believe me, I was on my way to see you. But I ran into Mr. Charles. He said that you asked for a transfer. Is that true?"

"Well, I was hurt by the way things happened, and I didn't think it would be a good idea to stay there and have so much tension between us," Monica explained.

Alvin cleared his throat and said, "Baby, is it alright for me to come over there and talk to you?"

"No, I don't think that would be a good idea right now. I prefer not to see you, but we can continue talking."

"I understand. I don't know how many times I am going to have to apologize, but I will do it a million times if it will get you to forgive me."

Monica started crying, "I trusted you with my heart Alvin. All my life it seems as though people just leave for one reason or another. I didn't want to be involved with anyone because I didn't want to go through any more hurt in my life. People just don't stay in my life. They either leave me, or just die. When I first started talking to you, I never could have imagined how much I was going to fall in love with you. It was like when you came into my life, all of my cloudy days turned to sunshine.

"You are a beautiful man Alvin, and I know that women are always going to throw themselves at you. I just expected you to be a whole lot stronger and understand how they will try and manipulate you. You said that nothing happened that day, but you have to understand it from my point of view. Your ex manipulated you to come over to her house without you even considering telling me."

"So to say that nothing happened is a gross understatement. How do I know if she wouldn't be able to make you do other things? Granted you told me that you kissed her on the cheeks, but how do I know if you are ever going to tell me the next time if you two were to hook to up for any other reasons?"

"I just want you to see that you've caused a problem in this relationship that I don't think can easily be repaired. I know you love me, you proved that by buying me a ring and wanting to marry me. But to be honest, I really don't think that I could ever forgive you for what you have done."

"Monica, I know it looked a little fucked up, but believe me baby, Keisha doesn't mean anything to me. I already told you that. My heart is yours and it will always belong to you. Please don't let this break up something special. There will never be another woman that I love more than you."

Monica stayed silent. Alvin began pleading and begging even more, but it all fell on deaf ears. In the end Monica said, "I do love you Alvin, But I don't want to be with you right now. Just give me some time and I might be able to forgive you."

Alvin was extremely heart broken, "I will give you the time that you need, but please don't have me waiting for you if you really don't want to be with me anymore. That is all I am going to ask of you."

Monica agreed and told Alvin that it wouldn't be good to see each other at work if they could help it.

"You know that is going to be hard to do, But I will do my best to stay away from your area."

They both said goodbye and hung up the phone. Weeks went by and Alvin noticed that nothing had changed in their relationship. He grew more and more frustrated as the days passed. He didn't want to impose on Monica's wishes, so he kept quiet and stayed away from her.

One day while at the office, Joseph saw that Alvin was in a really bad mood. He walked up to Alvin and said, "Hey boss, is everything okay?"

Alvin looked at him and snapped, "Why do you want to know, don't you have work to do?"

"Hold up partner, everyone around here knows what happened between you and Monica. I know that you are upset, but you can't be coming around here taking all of your frustration out on us because we didn't do anything to you."

Alvin smiled and said, "Damn, I've been that bad?"

Shaking his head Joseph said, "Hell yeah, I was about to go home and get my rifle and come back here just to put you out of your misery."

They both started laughing, "You just don't know man, I went out and bought this woman a nice rock and now it looks like we aren't ever going to be together. So hell yeah I'm pissed!"

Joseph put his arm around Alvin's neck and said, "Listen, I'm old school. When you fall off the horse, the best thing to do is get right back on it."

Chapter Five

Easing the Pain

Alvin nodded his head yes and continued to listen. Joseph told Alvin that he and a few guys from work were going to hang out later that night and asked if he would like to join. "You know what, I think that would be a good idea. It would truly help me to get my mind off of things."

"Now you're talking boss, we'll see you after work." Later that day Alvin met up with Joseph, Billy and Kevin. They went to this nice after work strip club and had a few drinks. They spent most of the night teasing Alvin about how whipped he was over Monica.

Billy said in a drunken voice, "I know that bitch is fine Alvin, but damn brother, don't let her control you with her tits in your mouth."

Alvin who was a little drunk himself, said, "Listen, these bitches up in here might be bitches, but don't you dare call my girl that shit!"

Joseph knew that things were getting a little out of hand, so he gave both Billy and Alvin some one-dollar bills and reminded them that they were there to have fun, not fight. Billy stood up and said, "You're right. I apologize to my man. Besides I need my God damn job!"

Alvin laughed and accepted Billy's apologies. Everyone started having a great time with the women in the club. After some time had passed, a woman came over to Alvin and said, "Damn daddy, you're fine as hell. Why you left your wife home to come be with me?"

Alvin turned toward the young lady to get a good look at her. "First off, let's get something straight, for one I'm not married. Secondly, I didn't even know you existed until you came over here."

The woman who was only wearing a red leather thong and matching bikini top started squeezing both of her breasts in front of Alvin's face and said, "Well let me introduce myself, my name is April and I would just love to give you a lap dance."

Alvin stared at April breasts all in his face and saw that April was the light skinned version of Monica. April had a very beautiful body. she too had long fake hair that was blonde and matched her light skin complexion perfectly. When he looked at her lips, he knew that they were the perfect lips for sucking. April turned around, putting her nice curvy butt in Alvin's face and said, "Come on big daddy let me wine on you."

Alvin was very tempted to grab April's butt. "No, I wouldn't feel right having you do that. Why don't you tell just me how a beautiful woman like yourself ended up here?"

"My boss is looking and if you want to talk, then you going to have to get the lap dance. Otherwise I am going to have to move on to the next customer."

"Okay, I'm curious to know a little something about you. Go ahead and do that dance!"

April turned toward Alvin and straddled across his lap, wining very slowly. She told Alvin to ask her anything he wanted to know.

"Well you could start off by answering the first question."

April, starting to moan when she felt that Alvin cock became erected. "Well I actually have a sad story big daddy; I don't think you want to hear that right now especially when little man is trying to bust of your pants."

"I'm actually paying more for the story than for the lap dance so make it good!" Alvin exclaimed.

April put Alvin's head into her breasts and started shaking them. "I left home when I was a teenager. I left because I was being abused by my father and cousins. When I left, I was on my own in the streets, doing whatever I could do to survive. One day a group of guys grabbed me and took me in a back ally and started to rape me repeatedly. When they were done, they punched and kicked me so hard I became unconscious. I didn't know if it was their plan to kill me or if they just got scared that I was already dead. Anyhow, the owner of this club found me and took me to the hospital.

"He paid all of my hospital bills and came to visit me whenever he could. In the end, he told me that I didn't have to repay him. He also told me that if I worked at his club he would make sure that no one ever hurt me again. Ten years later I'm still here. I have no regrets, the money is good, I have my own place, and I sure don't have to depend on any man!"

Alvin put on a sympathetic smiled and said in a drunken voice, "Damn, you just messed up my high with that story! I'm so sorry that you had a very rough life growing up."

"Well everyone can't have it easy like you big Daddy!" Alvin grabbed her around the neck and pulled her toward him. He gave her a passionate kiss as looked into her eyes.

"Nice to meet you Ms. April, my name is Alvin."

April enjoyed the kiss so much she started singing, "Alvin and April sitting on a stool, she grinding and wining making him drool. She grinded so hard she made him pop, but that didn't make this fine girl stop! I really love your name, but sorry, the lap dance is over. You owe me fifty dollars for the lap dance and you can give me a little extra for my story if you want to."

"What? Fifty dollars? You're lucky I happened to enjoy the story better than the lap dance."

Alvin pulled out his wallet and gave April a one-hundred-dollar bill. He also saw one of his cards in there and gave it to her. April looked at the card and said, "Why are you giving me this? You know I am not the kind of girl you would take home to your mother."

Alvin slowly started rubbing his hands up and down April's legs, "Perhaps, but you haven't heard my story yet, and if you ever are interested and want to hear my story, then you can give me a call to find out."

"Well big daddy, I will be getting off in an hour and I could use a ride home. Normally I would take a cab home, but you can tell me your story while you're dropping me off."

"That sounds nice, but I came here with the fellows. Besides, I'm too drunk to drive anything right now," Alvin admitted.

April looked at Alvin seductively and said, "I bet if I was to put you in my driver's seat you would be able to drive me without any problems."

Alvin then put his arms around April and smacked her on the butt saying, "I tell you what, when you get off from work, we both would get into a cab and go home together."

April started nodding her head in agreement, "I have to be honest with you Alvin. I have never gone home with anyone since I've been working here. For some reason I really like you and wouldn't mind being in your company. So with that said, whose house are we going to go to?"

Alvin said, "Hell I don't care, just as long as we get there."

"Well we will figure that out when the time comes," said April, easing her way off of Alvin. "Right now I have to go and mingle with a few more customers. It's almost time to go though, so please don't leave me. I'll come and get you when I'm done."

"Don't worry, I will be right here when you are done."

"Okay, but I better not see any other woman grinding on my stuff."

"It will all be right here just waiting for you."

April left to go mingle with the other customers. Joseph then came over immediately to Alvin and said, "Damn bro, that honey is much finer than Monica. I don't see how in the hell you be doing that."

"What are you talking about?" Alvin said, confused.

Joseph smirked at him and continued. "Keisha, fine as hell. Then you get Monica, who is much finer than Keisha. Now you walk up in here and you were with that hot babe for what seemed like hours. Did you get her number?"

"I did better than that. I am going home with her in a few minutes."

Joseph started slapping Alvin five and said with a drunken, loud voice said, "My dog! There's a player in the house."

Alvin looked at him and said, "Shhhh, you know there are a lot of haters around."

When April was finished she came to Alvin and told him that she was ready. Alvin went to his co-workers and introduced April. He told them that he wasn't going to ride home with them and that he'd see them in the office on Monday. All of them had little childish grins on their faces as they wished Alvin the best of luck.

While they were outside, Alvin and April agreed to go to his place since it was closer. When they got there, April stepped into his house and said, "I'm glad we decided to come to your place, because my place looks like crap compared to this."

Alvin took April's overcoat and saw that she was just wearing the same outfit underneath it. He offered April something to drink, but she declined, "After being in that dark nasty club all night, all I want to do is take a nice hot shower to get some of those nasty men off of me."

Alvin pulled her closer up to him "Well excuse me, I happen to be one of those men dear!"

April laughed and said, "I know, that's why I think you should come join me in the shower."

Alvin took April to his bathroom and they started removing each other's clothes. When they stepped into the shower, they slowly started washing each other. Alvin then pushed April into the wall and started grinding on her like she did for him in the club. Hard as a rock, April took advantage and went down on Alvin. She kept at it until Alvin wasn't able to take it anymore. He lifted her up and bent her down in front of him.

As the water continued to bead on their body, Alvin started pounding April doggy style. Her head kept hitting the wall slightly, but she moaned with every stroke. Without any worries, Alvin climaxed inside of April and then picked her up and carried her to the bedroom while they were still soaking wet. Alvin then laid her on the bed and began kissing all over April until he reached her vagina. April grew wild as he licked and sucked on her clit. It wasn't long before April let out a scream saying that she was going to cum all over his face.

Alvin stayed there until April exploded and did exactly that, she came all over his face. It was dripping everywhere. That turned Alvin on so much that he was ready to go at it again. He got on top of April, but this time he was very passionate with her. He slowly slid in and out of her, kissing her very softly with each stroke. Again, Alvin couldn't control himself and climaxed even harder inside of April. Afterwards he rolled over and laid on his back.

April turned toward him and laid her head on Alvin's chest. April said, "I don't know who you thought you were making love to, but that was the first time a man ever made love to me like that. I really felt an energy that I've never felt before."

Alvin replied, "I must confess, you remind me of my ex in so many ways. I was actually thinking about her when we were here in the bedroom. Don't get me wrong though, I was definitely enjoying making love to you. There were just a few times that I was thinking that you were her."

April looked up at Alvin and said, "That's okay big daddy; she must have been a wonderful woman for you to make love to her like that. I'm not mad at you. It's been a while for me since I even let myself let a man take control of my body the way that you just did. I have to admit, I totally enjoyed every bit of it. As you can see, you still have my body shaking."

"Well she's a major part of my story and I am still very much in love with her. I really messed things up between us. I'm sure you are smart enough to know how the story goes."

April smiled and said, "Yes I know. Men just can't keep their little thingy in their pants. Not to say that you're little, you are definitely far from that. But damn keep it in your pants!"

"See you don't even know what happened; It was nothing like that," Alvin said, with a little harshness in his voice. He got on top of April and said, "Besides, you weren't complaining when I was breaking your back and you were screaming and cumming all over the place."

April started smiling, "Yes, but if you weren't digging another woman's back out, then I wouldn't be here. Your woman would be here instead."

Alvin sucked his teeth and rolled off of her. "For your information I didn't have sex with the other woman. My woman was just mad because I went to my ex's house to fix her computer without letting her know where I was going to be."

April then climbed on top of Alvin, "Let me get this straight, she left some good stuff just because you didn't check in? I don't know her, but it sounds to me like she has some other issues going on there."

Alvin nodded his head and said, "Yes, she might be just a little insecure, but it's all for a good reason."

"I'm sorry Alvin but she's a stupid bitch. Does she know how hard it is to find a good man? Not to mention that you also look good and have a nice paying job. I know I only knew you for a few hours, but I could tell that you were a gentleman the minute we started talking. I'll say damn, fuck her. Since you said I reminded you a little bit of her, why you don't just get with me?"

"Don't take this the wrong way, I really do like you. When it came to the sex it was fantastic, but we are from two different worlds. It would never work between us."

April's face turned serious and she rolled her eyes at Alvin "So you think 'once a whore always a whore'? That I couldn't be that woman you take home to your mother. Well fuck you!"

Alvin put his arms around April's waist "Listen, I didn't mean it like that. I'm sure that you have a lot of man issues that you really need to get help with before you can honestly see yourself in a productive relationship."

April removed Alvin's arms and rolled off of him. "That's okay I get it, I'm good enough to fuck, but I'm not good enough to be any man's wife." She stood up and started putting on her clothes. She then asked Alvin to call her a cab. During the whole time that she was getting dressed, Alvin didn't say a word. He didn't want to offer her a ride home because he knew it would have been a very long, awkward ride.

While they both stood in his living room waiting for the cab, Alvin said, "Nothing for nothing, I just want you to know that I do think that you are a very beautiful woman. I really wish that you didn't do the type of work that you do."

The expression of disgust showed on April face, "Whatever, at least I'm taking care of myself by myself and I don't need any trick niggers like you trying to make himself feel good by fucking what he thinks is a whore. So don't get it twisted, I'm not that whore who you think I am. I have never gone home with any customers from that place. You were my first one and my last!"

Right at that moment the cab came and April left. Feeling a little down, Alvin then gave Keisha a call. Keisha answered the phone knowing that it was Alvin and said, "Well stranger, long time no hear."

Alvin replied, "I know, it's been a while since I've talked to you. How've you been?"

"A lot has been happening with me over the past few weeks. I'm actually somewhat in a relationship right now."

Alvin, although a little disappointed with the news, tried to sound happy, "Wow Keisha, I am really happy for you."

"Well you know he's not an Alvin, but he's pretty close to you, so I'm very satisfied."

"Why would you be looking for someone like me?"

"Because I never felt the love of a man like you, and I guess because I am still somewhat in love with you. I wanted someone who could make me feel the way that you did."

Alvin said, "Wow, I am honored."

Keisha then tried to change the subject. "So how are you and Monica working out? Did you two patch things up and get back together?"

Alvin took a deep breath before answering, "Well, we are pretty much where we left off a few weeks ago. If you ask me, I don't think that we will ever get back together again."

After a brief pause, Keisha said, "Gee Alvin, I'm really feeling bad that I had something to do with you two breaking up. I actually wish that I could turn back the hands of time for you because you are such a wonderful guy. I know how much you loved her."

"It's okay, I used to blame you but deep down I know it's my entire fault."

"Well I also know that I messed up with you. Deep down in my heart, I will always try to be the best friend you could ever have. I really sincerely mean that Alvin."

Alvin felt a sadness that came over him, "To be honest Keisha, I never really fell out of love with you. Granted I don't like what you have done, but I should have forgiven you and given you another chance."

Keisha smiled and let out a little chuckle, "See that's just like you Alvin, now you're talking about giving me another chance after I went out and found another you"

"I wasn't talking about giving you another chance now. I was talking about when things were actually messed up. I do value you more as my friend now than when you were my lover."

Keisha sucked her teeth and said "Whatever, you know you still want to hit this. I don't know why you are acting like you don't miss this sweet stuff. I guess now that you know that I am with someone else, you understand that you can't touch this anymore."

Alvin started laughing, "Keisha, it really doesn't matter who you are with. If I still wanted some of that,

I know what I have to do to get it. Besides I was being very serious about having you as a friend. In that regard, you are very special to me."

The tone of Keisha's voice became serious, "I was only playing with you Alvin. Believe it or not, I love having you as a friend as well."

They continued to talk for a few more hours. Mainly it was about Keisha and her new man. Afterwards they said goodbye to each other and then called it a night.

Chapter Six

Second Chances

The next day while Alvin was sitting in his office, he received a surprise visit from Monica. Alvin thought to himself that she looked as beautiful as ever. She walked in with a big smile on her face and said, "I bet you didn't expect to see me here right?"

Alvin, who was also sporting a big grin on his face said, "Yes, you are absolutely correct, you caught me totally off guard."

Monica walked up to his desk and laid a chicken salad on it.

"I was thinking about you today and wanted to bring you lunch like the good old days, is that okay?"

"If you would have just walked up in here with nothing in your hands and told me that you were thinking about me, I would have been just as happy," Alvin said, beaming.

"Well just consider this as a peace offering, and if it's alright with you, I would like to come over to your place tonight so that we can talk."

Alvin, with an even bigger grin on his face, said, "Now that's the best news I've heard all week. Thank you for the salad and I will see you let's say around eight?"

Monica nodded her head yes, walked over to Alvin and gave him a kiss on the forehead.

"Wow, thank you. That was both pleasant and unexpected."

"Well that was just to let you know how much you were missed. I'll see you at eight."

After Monica left, Joseph came over to Alvin's desk and said, "I see that big smile on your face boss man, does that mean you are back in there?"

Alvin just shrugged his shoulders and lifted his hands up in the air, "She brought me lunch and asked to come over tonight, so I really don't know what to expect."

"It sounds like another chance to me. You better not mess it up this time boss man. I'll be watching!"

Alvin gave Joseph a light punch on the shoulders and said, "You better believe that's not going to happen. Not in a million years!"

Alvin was extremely excited for the rest of the day. Later that night Monica arrived at Alvin's house. While letting her in, Alvin said, "You look very beautiful as always."

"Thank you" Monica replied, and headed for the sofa.

Monica motioned Alvin to come sit next to her. When Alvin sat down Monica said, "Okay, I am not going to sugar coat anything. I am just going to tell you what's on my mind and let you take it from there."

Alvin, being a gentleman said, "Would you like for me to fix you anything before you start?"

"No, I just want you to sit here and pay attention to what I have to say."

Alvin sat next to Monica with big puppy eyes and said, "Okay, you have my undivided attention."

Monica reached over and took one of Alvin's hands, "I know you told me that nothing happened that day and I really believe you, but I just didn't like the way you went about it. I had some time to think about everything and decided to give us another chance."

Alvin lifted up Monica's hand and kissed it as he closed his eyes. "Baby, I'm so sorry about everything that I have done to hurt you. Deep in my heart you are the only woman I ever want to be with and I will do my best to make you feel that way with every breath in my body."

Monica put her arms around Alvin's neck, placed her forehead on top of his and started crying. "You don't know how hard it's been everyday thinking about you and wanting to be with you. From what I can remember, I never loved a man the way I love you Alvin. I just for once in my life want to be happy and forget about all the bad things that happened to me."

Alvin pulled back, reached into his pocket and pulled out the engagement ring. "When I got you this, it was me making a commitment not only to you, but to myself that I will love you and only you for the rest of my life. There isn't any other woman in the world that would make me change my mind about that."

Alvin then got on one knee and said, "Monica, would you please give me the satisfaction and honor of being your husband?"

Monica put on the ring and said, "Yes, I would really love to be your wife."

Alvin reached up and pulled Monica to the floor where he made love to her throughout the night. The next day both Monica and Alvin walked into the firm arm-in-arm. Anyone who saw and stopped them, Monica would hold up the hand with the ring on it and say, "We're engaged!"

Both of them then separated and went to their offices. Alvin saw Mr. Charles talking to Joseph in his office. He walked up to them and said, "Today my good friends, I'm turning in my player's card."

Mr. Charles looked at Joseph and said, "See this is why I don't want anyone drinking on the job, what is he talking about?"

"You know what boss, that sounds like a great idea. We need to celebrate my engagement to the beautiful Ms. Monica!"

Mr. Charles shook Alvin's hands and said, "Congratulations, I always thought you two would make a great couple."

Joseph had a sideway smile, but he was very happy about the news, "Man you're lucky, I was going to give you one more week to try and fix things up, and then I was going in."

Alvin laughed, "Man please, she would have left you standing right there out in the cold!"

"Yeah your right man, you have my deepest congrats."

Chapter Seven

Good News, Bad News

Weeks went by and everything was going great with Alvin and Monica. One day while Alvin was sitting at home, he got a call from April. Alvin answered, "Hey you, I didn't expect to hear from you anymore. How are you doing?"

"I was wondering why you never called me back. You didn't even have the decency to check and make sure that I made it home safe that night. I guess I was just a one-night booty call to you huh?"

"No. It wasn't like that, and I really do apologize for not checking in on you. I actually thought that we really did vibe that night, and then it got a little out of control. On top of all of that, my woman and I got back together and I was really concentrating on making everything work out with her."

April sucked her teeth and said, "So the bitch finally came to her senses and decided to give you another chance?"

"Don't call her that. You don't know anything about her. She is someone that really means a lot to me and I would really appreciate it if you didn't call her that," Alvin snapped.

"Oh so fuck me, I'm nothing to you but a booty call and you don't have to respect me or my feelings right?"

Alvin started laughing and said, "April, you're a very nice woman and I'm sorry if you feel the way that you do. But to be honest, I really don't need this kind of drama in my life right now. What in the hell did you call me for?"

April whole body turned red and in a nasty voice she said, "Fuck you, you should have thought about all that shit when you brought me home that fucking day."

Alvin grew angry and said in a loud tone, "Listen, first of all, I don't know why you are doing all of this cursing. Secondly, you're right, it is what it is. It was a one-night stand. You're just going to have to accept it for what it was and move on. I really don't want anything to do with you anymore, and I would appreciate it if you never ever call me again.

April became furious, "No you listen to me. I'm getting sick and tired of men acting like their shit doesn't stink. Did you think you could just treat women any kind of way and then dispose of us like garbage?"

Alvin replied, "That wasn't my intention, but look at where we met. Did you honestly think that I was going to be with you after one night of sex? Again, it is what it is. So please don't call me anymore and have a good life."

April tone and behavior became uncontrollable, "Fuck you! You better tell your fucking bitch that you have a baby on the way and I'm keeping it!"

April hung up the phone. Alvin was stung. He tried calling April back but the calls were going straight to her voice mail. Alvin's rage started to grow the more he thought about the situation. He started picking up things in his house and throwing them onto the walls. Just before he was about to totally lose his mind, Keisha called.

He picked up the phone and in a calm voice said, "Hello Keisha, now isn't a good time to talk."

"Is everything alright Alvin? I just called to tell you some good news".

Alvin took a deep breath and said, "Okay, I guess I could use some good news at this point."

"Well, the guy that I am seeing proposed to me yesterday. I'm getting married. Isn't that great news?"

Alvin cleared his throat and said, "Didn't you just started seeing this guy? You barely even know him."

Keisha said, "Yes, but I think I love him enough to want to settle down with him."

Alvin shook his head in disapproval and said, "Well if you think he's going to make you happy, then I guess the only thing I can do is be happy for you."

Keisha, not sounding too happy about Alvin's response, said, "Wow, I thought you would sound a little bit happier for me. Besides, I actually left out the best part. We're going to have a baby. I'm going to be a mother!"

Alvin started laughing hysterically, "What the hell is going on? Is it baby making season or what?"

"What are you talking about Alvin? Because right now I'm really starting to regret even calling you."

"I'm sorry, it's just that right before you called, this chick I met told me that she was pregnant and that I was the father."

"Well I don't understand, didn't you wanted to find someone to have a family with? You should be happy."

"No! She was just a one-night stand that I met at the strip club. I could never see myself being married to that. Besides, Monica and I just got back together and we are engaged."

In a disappointing low tone Keisha said, "What? You and Monica got back together and now you are finding out that you have a baby on the way with another woman? Damn Alvin, how could you be so stupid to have sex with a woman you just met at a strip club and not protect yourself?"

"I know, I know, I was drinking heavily that night and to be honest I really didn't care at the time because I was in a bad frame of mind. I wanted to feel like it was real love, but getting her pregnant was the last thing on my mind."

Keisha took a deep breath and said, "So what do you plan to do now Alvin? If you want my opinion, I think you should tell Monica about the situation and give her a choice about where things should go. After what happened the first time between you two, I really don't think keeping this away from her would be a good idea."

Alvin sucked his teeth and said, "Please, I don't even know if she is actually pregnant or if the kid is mine. Why should I put my relationship with Monica in jeopardy again when we just got back together? No, I'm sorry. I couldn't go through the emotion of losing Monica again. She means much too much to me and I don't ever want to lose her again."

"So what do you plan on doing Alvin?

"I would make her take the paternity test after she has the baby, and then I could decide what to do from there. If the baby is not mine than all would be good. If the baby is mine, then I guess I will have to cross that bridge when it comes."

"I don't know Alvin. I think you are playing with fire by not telling Monica the truth now. If she was so upset with you just because you came and fixed my computer, I can't imagine how much of an impact it would have on her if she knew you had a baby on the way and didn't tell her."

"Yes I know, that is the exact reason why I can't tell her. I already learned my lesson by being too truthful the first time. Besides, nine months from now I'm sure our relationship would be strong enough to handle this or any situation."

"Well you know I love you enough to hope that everything works out in your favor. Nine months from now I'm going to be a mother and a wife. I am very excited to have that family I always wanted. I hope one day you get to meet my future husband."

Alvin smiled and said,

"Gee, my news was so grim I forgot about your happiness for a moment. I am truly happy for you Keisha and of course I am wishing you a happy, healthy new life."

"Aw thank you Alvin, I really appreciate you supporting me like this. I was actually afraid that you were going to flip out on me."

"No, I couldn't do that," said Alvin. "What kind of friend would I be if I couldn't be happy for you with such great news?" I'm going to always be in your corner."

Once again Keisha had a big smile on her face and told Alvin that she hoped his situation would turn out the way he wanted it to. They both said their goodbyes and hung up the phone. Right after they hung up, Alvin tried calling April back again. Again the call went straight to her voice mail.

Alvin then called Monica and asked if she wanted to go away for the weekend just to make plans for a wedding. Monica was all smiles and agreed. That weekend while they were away, Alvin struggled with the notion of telling Monica the truth. Later that evening while out having dinner, Monica grew suspicious and asked Alvin if was he okay.

Alvin said, "I was just thinking about something and wanted to know the answer to this burning question that has been bothering me all day."

Monica replied, "Sure you can ask me anything sugar bear."

"Sugar bear? Is that the nickname you have picked out for me?"

"Because you are so sweet to me and such a nice cuddle bear, yes that is the name that I've chosen for you," Monica said, beaming.

Alvin smiled and said, "Okay, I like it. It has a very nice ring to it. When I come up with a nickname for you, you will be the first one to know."

"I will be waiting dear, now ask me the question that been bothering you."

Alvin leaned forwarded, grabbed Monica's hands and said, "Do you want a big wedding or a small one?"

"Baby you know when it comes to family, I basically do not have any. So this day is going to be just as special for you as it is for me. Whatever you decide would be alright with me."

"I have family and friends, but I just don't want it to be all one sided. I was just thinking about having something small," Alvin said, while squeezing Monica's hands.

"Aww you are so sweet dear! That is why I love you so much. To be honest I don't care we if we have a big wedding or a small one, just as long as I'm with you forever."

Alvin gazed into Monica's eyes "I never want to lose you ever again. You mean absolutely the world to me. I am so ready for us to become one and have a family."

Monica smiled and said, "Really! I actually didn't think you wanted kids."

Alvin puckered his lips and leaned forwarded, giving Monica a big wet kiss on the lips. "With you, I would want to have an army of kids."

They continued to talk and eat until it was time to leave the restaurant. When they got back to their room, they made passionate love the whole weekend. Later that Sunday night, Alvin took Monica home and told her that he wasn't going to spend the rest of the night with her. Monica told him that she had a big court case in the morning and needed the rest anyway. They kissed and hugged and then Alvin headed home.

When Alvin arrived home, he found a positive pregnancy test in his mailbox with a letter from April. He went inside, sat down. and started reading the letter.

"Dear Alvin,

I know you were probably thinking that I was lying to you about being pregnant. Well here is the proof. I know you only think about me as a stripper whore, but I am far from that. I meant it when I said you were the only guy that I've ever gone home with. Since I am about to be the mother of your child, I want you to know that I am really a good woman.

To prove that to you, I quit my job at the strip club yesterday. You should know that was really hard for me to do considering that I've worked there for most of my life. I really need you to know and believe that I am much more than that Alvin.

A few years ago I went to school and got my license to become a beautician. The money was so good at the club and I never thought about doing hair full time until now. So since I already have my license, I took a job at my friend's salon who has been asking me to work for her for years.

Of course, the money is going to be much tighter now, but I'm willing to do whatever it takes to have my child respect me as a mother. I also wanted to let you know the reason why I am keeping this baby is because I always wanted to have a child, but I never was able to get pregnant. So this little bundle to me is like my miracle child. I know I could never be like your girlfriend, but I am willing to do whatever it takes to make my family whole.

Sometimes I'm hard to deal with, I also know that I can be a little street at times. That's just who I am. I felt so alive when you made love to me that night, I wanted it to be that way forever with you. I'm willing to set aside our differences in the hopes that you can consider me as someone that you could settle down with. I really would love for you to come home to our baby and me and be that strong positive black man that I always wanted and needed in my life.

I also know that this might be a bit much that I am asking you for right now, but please think about it and give me a call to let me know how you feel about what I'm asking you.

P.S. I know that I am not able to say that I love you now, but I am hoping that one day we will be able to say it to each other in the near future…Smooches."

Alvin threw the letter down to the floor and started loudly saying, "Fuck!" repeatedly. He picked up the phone and started to call April, but he quickly put it back down. Alvin then picked up the letter and placed it in his drawer. He went to bed and stared at the walls all night wondering what to do.

Chapter Eight

Take My Advice

The next day Alvin pulled Joseph to the side and told him what happened.

"Damn, I knew you were going to fuck April, but why didn't you use a condom?"

"Man I wasn't in the right frame of mind that night. I guess I was so angry that Monica and I weren't talking that I just didn't care at the time. Plus, when you add in the drinking, that just made a bad situation worse. Now she's telling me that she wants us to be a family. I'm telling you man, I think that girl is a little twisted."

"See, you go around putting it on these women and now you can't get rid of them. If you want my opinion, I would just go ahead and tell Monica now. It would be much easier for her to know now way before the baby gets here rather than after."

Alvin raised his voice and said, "Hell no! You don't understand how hard it was trying to gain Monica's trust and love again. I'm not going through that again."

Joseph looked at Alvin and shook his head. "You have to understand how women think my brother. You just can't go around with something heavy like that and think that it's going to go away. Did I ever tell you why my wife and I, after fifteen years of marriage, divorced? To be honest it was the same situation that you find yourself in right now. She was a beautiful woman just like your Monica. Man let me tell you, every night when I got home, dinner was always on the table. We had what you might call that old school marriage. We prayed together and wept together. We actually could damn near finish each other's sentences. That was how in tune we were with one another.

"One day on my way home, I started noticing this hooker hanging out by my way. Now for a street walker she was alright, but not the kind of woman you would throw a marriage away over you understand. Anyway, every day I would start seeing this woman more and more. Of course when that happens you get to know them well enough to start saying *hi*. So as time passed, every day that I saw her I would walk by and we would exchange greetings. Of course I would just keep it moving because I really didn't want anyone to see me talking to her for too long. You know how people get. They might get the wrong idea and start spreading stuff that isn't true.

"One day when I was coming home, I saw a man get out of his car and punch her so hard in the face that she was knocked out. Before I could reach where they were, he got back into his car and took off, leaving her lying there on the sidewalk. I pulled out my cell phone and called for help. By the way when she was laying down there, I actually thought that she was dead. I tried to do whatever I could to revive her, but I was unsuccessful. When the ambulance and police finally came they ask me if I knew her. I told them that I would see her here every day and say hi to her, but I actually didn't know anything about her or who she was.

"They asked me could I ride with her because she didn't have any ID on her and it would be very helpful to explain to the police what I saw. So I agreed and called my wife and told her what happened. I also told her that I was going to be home late for dinner because the police wanted me to ride to the hospital with her and ask me a few questions. She said, 'That's my husband, always helping out complete strangers.' We both laughed and I got into the ambulance.

"While in the emergency ward, the poor woman came to and asked me what happened and how did she get here. I told her the story and she said, 'That fucking asshole is going to pay dearly for this shit.' So I told her my name and she told me that her name was Linda. I told her that I wasn't here to judge her, but asked why she was into the life style that she was in.

"With a grunt of pain, she said, 'Because I dropped out of school when I was eleven. I ran away from home because my father sexually assaulted me and my mother was too high on crack to even notice. I had a couple of pimps in my lifetime, but after getting beatings and starving to death because I didn't see any of the money I made, I just decided to get away and moved here. With no skill or education, I was forced to do what I know in order to survive on my own.' Man I tell you, when she told me that story, I was like *damn* just when you think you have it bad, someone comes along and tops you tenfold."

Alvin interrupted and said, "I don't see how that messed up your marriage."

Joseph started again, "After she got out of the hospital our relationship changed. I was concerned about her wellbeing more and more, like a father. Every time I would see her, now we would talk a little bit more than usual. After a while we became really great friends. I do have to admit during that time I was starting to look at her a little differently. One day on my way home, she insisted on me stopping by her place and having dinner with her. Basically she said that she never thanked me for saving her life and just wanted to show her appreciation.

"Of course I told her that she didn't owe me anything. Just as long as she was alright, that was good enough for me. But she was like 'Come on, I know you want to get home to your wife, I promise I will not keep you long.' Since I knew she wasn't going to take no for an answer, I just agreed and told her only for a few minutes. When we got to her place it was very nice, you could tell that she was a very clean woman who took pride in how her place looked. If you ask me, I think she respected her home well enough not to allow any of her johns to come there. It almost looked like it was her place to escape from the hard life and madness she was so used to. Anyway, she took my coat and asked me to have a seat. She then asked if I wanted to have something to drink. I told her no because I sure didn't want my wife to know that I was drinking before I got home.

"She poured herself a drink and pulled out some nice golden fried chicken and some macaroni and cheese that were warming up in the oven. Man let me tell you, that woman knew how to throw down in the kitchen! But to make a long story short, eventually we did start sleeping together and like you, being careless, she got pregnant. I kept it a secret from my wife for over two years until one day Linda was found dead in an ally. No one actually knew who killed her. The cops stopped searching for her killer because no one came forward and there was not enough evidence to convict anyone.

"I cried so much because I really was in love with that woman. I also didn't know where my son was. He was my little junior and my only child. After I found out that she died, I went to the day care center where she normally takes him and found out that the department of child services already took him. I've been searching for him ever since. You know they make it kind of hard when your name isn't on the birth certificate.

"To this day, ten years later, I still don't know where he is or even if he's still alive. Eventually it all started to take a toll on me. I was grieving so much over her death and losing my son, I had to tell my wife what was going on because at that time I was a total mess. My wife was angry and heartbroken because we tried for years to have a kid and it never happened. It's like no matter how hard you ask a person to forgive you, if they are feeling a certain way toward you, it will never happen. She would say that every time she looked at me, it would remind her of the situation. She later divorced me and died five years ago of breast cancer.

"The Doctors said that they could have saved her, but she kept refusing the treatments. I tried very hard to be there during her last days, but she never really let me back into her life. Trust me, if I could do it all over again I would have never hurt that woman the way I did. I've done so many things wrong in my past, the best thing I can do now is ask for God's forgiveness. So as you see my brother, because you are not married now, I think you owe it to Monica to give her that choice."

Alvin put his arms around Joseph and said, "I'm so sorry for all that you have lost. I must say that you've taught me a very valuable lesson today."

Joseph said, "What's that?" Alvin replied, "April's story is somewhat like Linda's story. She really doesn't deserve to be treated the way that I've been treating her either. I am going to try my best to improve on the way I've been talking to her. Actually I think I'm going to call her later because I've been trying to avoid her like she was the plague lately. I'm also going to tell Monica the truth about what is going on as well, even though I know that would probably be the end of our relationship."

Joseph's face lit up and he said, "Now you are starting to sound like a real man making real decisions."

Later that night when Alvin got home, Alvin picked up the phone and called April. In a very seductive voice, April said, "Hi Alvin, I am so glad that you called me. I thought I scared you away with the letter and pregnancy test that I left in your mailbox."

"Listen April, I really don't want this conversation to head south so please pay close attention. This is what we are going to do. It's not that I don't believe you or anything, but I'm going to buy another pregnancy test and you are going to take it while I'm standing there. Secondly, I know you want me to be a part of your life but right now that isn't going to happen. I'm not saying that I wouldn't be there for you or the baby if it is mine. I'm just saying that as for us being a couple, that isn't going to happen anytime soon."

April interrupted Alvin and said, "But you are not saying we would never be a couple, you're saying just not now right?"

"Yes, I guess if you want to put it that way. But Like it or not, for me to even think about having anything to do with you, it will all depend on how my woman Monica takes this situation."

April said, "Monica! Hmm so in other words, I will just be the rebound chick that just so happens to be having your baby. How do you think that is making me feel?"

Alvin shot back, "Please, like I said in the beginning, I don't want this conversation to go south. Just try to respect what I'm saying to you and let's work to be civil toward each other for the baby's sake."

April was silent for a few seconds and said, "Okay Alvin, I am going to do whatever you say because in the end, I know you are going to be a good father and do whatever you can to be a family with me and our baby. So when would you like for me to take the test?"

Alvin sighed and said, "This weekend would be fine. I could come by your place around three on Saturday if that's okay with you."

April, sounding very happy and excited said, "Okay honey, I am looking forward to seeing you on Saturday at 3 p.m. Smooches."

They both said goodbye and hung up. Alvin immediately picked up the phone again and called Keisha. Keisha picked up her phone and said, "ALVIN! I was just thinking about you. What's going on with you dear?"

"Well Keisha it's about to go down this weekend. Saturday I am going to April's house to personally give her another pregnancy test. If she tests positive, then Sunday I am going to go to Monica's house and at least let her know what is going on."

"I am so proud of you Alvin for making the right decision. I know you must be struggling about telling Monica the truth, but in the end you will realize that you have made the right choice. See that is why I still love you so much. I think that you are the only real man standing these days beside my babe of course. By the way, our wedding is planned for June 21st, do you think you will be able to make it?"

"I wouldn't feel comfortable considering that I am your ex. It would feel kind of funny watching you getting married to another man."

"That's only because deep down you know you messed up and still want me," Keisha joked. "I'm just playing with you Alvin. I told you that you are my friend for life and as my friend I want you to share and be a part of my happiness."

"I understand, don't worry I will be there because I really do love you and appreciate you as a friend."

"Thank you very much Alvin, that really means a lot to me. I also want to wish you good luck this weekend with the ladies Alvin. I hope for your sake that it all goes according to how you would want it to go."

"Thank you Keisha. For what's it worth, I think I really did let the wrong woman get away. I value your friendship even more now than when we first started down this road."

"Aww Thank you Alvin. You always know exactly what to say to make a woman feel all vulnerable." They both hung up and Alvin then called Monica.

Monica answered the phone saying, "Alvin my love, how was your day my dear? Sorry I was out of the office today; This court case is kicking my butt. The guy that I am defending is guilty as shit, but he doesn't want to take any deals that the D.A. is putting on the table. So sugar bear, I could really use some *me time* with my man this weekend."

"Well that is the reason why I am calling you. I wanted to come over on Sunday and talk to you about a few things."

"What's going on with you, you don't sound too happy. Is everything alright?" Monica replied.

"Everything is just fine. I just wanted to sit down and talk about a few things with my lovely dovely. That's my new nickname for you."

Monica laughed and said, "Okay, a little weird, but I guess I could get use to that. But I was more hoping that we could spend the whole weekend together!"

"I know it would be really nice to do that, but I have something really important to take care of on Saturday."

"And what might that be? I know you are not trying to keep secrets from me already dear, right?"

"I assure you that everything will come to light on Sunday," Alvin promised.

"Okay I guess I will have to wait until then. What time do you think you will be stopping by?"

"I will come by sometime early in the afternoon, probably around noon."

Monica said, "Okay noon would be good for me. Good night my love, I love you always."

Alvin replied, "I will always love you as well my dear, I will talk to you tomorrow."

They both hung up and Alvin exhaled with a big sigh of relief. When Saturday came, Alvin showed up at April's house. When April opened the door she grabbed Alvin around the waist and gave him a kiss on the lips. Alvin was very surprised by her actions, but he didn't respond back. April then pulled him into her home and said, "I am so happy to see you Alvin. I really missed you."

Alvin looked at April's hot body and thought to himself *what in the world am I doing here*? He grabbed her hands and said, "I am very happy that you have agreed to do this. I don't want it to seem as though that I am calling you a liar, I just really wanted to make sure for myself that it's true."

Alvin reached into his coat pocket and pulled out the pregnancy test. "Here, this is for you." He handed April the pregnancy test and told her to take the test whenever she was ready.

"There is nothing more I want right now then to prove to you that I am carrying your child. So let's go do it now!"

She took the test and went into the bathroom, leaving the bathroom door open so that Alvin could see everything that she was doing. When she took off her panties she threw them at Alvin and said, "You know you want to take that home to remind you of sweet little o' me!"

April proceeded taking the test. When she was done, she handed Alvin the positive test results and said, "See I told you I was pregnant, just like I'm telling you that I am one hundred percent sure that it's yours. That's because I haven't been with anyone else just prior to you."

She flushed the toilet and bent over the sink exposing her bare butt toward Alvin. "It's a shame that you only tapped this ass once Alvin. Now that I am having your child, you know you can come and get it anytime you want."

She turned around and noticed that Alvin was starting to become erected. He just stood there for a moment and said, "Listen, I'm not here for all of that. I just wanted to get this first part out of the way and discuss what we are going to do now."

April walked closer to Alvin, softly grabbed his erection and said, "Yeah Alvin, what would you like to do now?"

Alvin started pushing April away but not hard enough to move her from his body. Alvin said, "April stop it. I mean it, I really don't want to hurt you."

With one hand on his cock she used the other one to lift up his shirt. Again Alvin tried pushing her away, but again not hard enough as she started caressing his nipples and then sucking on them. She also managed to pull down his zipper and grabbed his raw hard cock into her hands.

Alvin yelled, "What the fuck are you doing?" Even after saying those words, Alvin knew that he had become helpless as April stooped down and started sucking on his cock. At that point he totally stopped resisting as he began to move his hips with April's sucking motion. April knew that she had Alvin where she wanted him because he started to moan louder and louder. April turned around again and while she held Alvin's cock in one hand, she bent over and put it inside of her.

Alvin was mad about the situation, but couldn't help how good it felt being deep inside of April. He started pounding her harder and harder letting her know how upset he was. But with every stroke she just moaned and asked for him to give it to her even harder. Alvin then started to moan and April stopped him and escorted him to the bedroom.

Alvin mumbled to himself, "I can't believe I'm about to do this shit." April removed all of Alvin's clothes and laid him on the bed. She climbed on top of him and placed his cock inside of her again. Slowly she worked her hips on him and started talking to him in the process.

"Alvin, I want to give you this pussy anytime you want it. I miss having you deep inside of me baby. If you keep fucking me like this, we are going to have a lot of kids. Oh Alvin make this pussy yours baby, Make this pussy yours! I'm about to cum so hard on your cock baby. Oh yeah Alvin fuck me! Here it comes, here it comes baby, oh yesss!"

Alvin was enjoying everything that April was saying. All Alvin could say was, "Fuck, shit, this fucking pussy is so good. I can't believe I'm doing this shit. Oh shit, fuck, dammit. You are going to make me cum all up in your fucking pussy again."

Oh yes baby, fuck me, I'm cumming too."

They climaxed together and April fell off of Alvin and wrapped her arms around him. While playing with the hairs on his chest April said, "Now I don't feel like I'm a one night stand anymore."

Alvin kept quiet. All he could do was look at the ceiling in disbelief. "Alvin I'm not sorry about what just happened. Like I told you before, I want you to be a part of my life, a part of our lives. I want us to be a family more than anything."

Alvin turned to April and said, "What just happened will never happen again. I don't know why but I feel like I just got violated."

April moved her arms off of Alvin and in a loud tone said, "Excuse me! Are you fucking kidding me right now? Are you trying to say that you didn't enjoy what just happened?"

"The problem is I enjoyed it more than I should of have. Actually what I am saying is, it shouldn't have happened in the first place. I told you that I was engaged to be married to Monica, so why would you do that?"

"No you never told me that you were engaged to her. But you know what Alvin, you are a really nice guy, but sometimes you can be a real fucked up asshole! I'm really trying to be nice, but I have to tell you that my hormones are telling me to say fuck you and Monica. I changed my job and tried everything within my power to let you know that I want this. How can you not see that Alvin?"

Alvin rolled over on top of April, looked into her eyes and said, "I really do appreciate everything that you are doing for me and our child, but you also have to look at this situation from my point of view. I do not love you. The woman that I do love would probably hate me forever because of a mistake that I have made. That's something that I have to deal with right now. I'm about to have a child out of wedlock which goes against everything that I believe in. Trust me, I am so sexually attracted to you. I actually do have some feelings for you. But how do you think we can be together when there are so many things that say we shouldn't?"

April, with a tear falling from her eye said, "Because it wasn't a mistake to me when I came home with you that night. It wasn't a mistake to me that I was blessed to become pregnant by you. It wasn't a mistake to me when you came to the strip club and we ended up at your place. It wasn't a mistake to me that you were having problems with your girl Monica at the time. To me everything is happening because it was meant to happen. To me this is all God's plan, and if you can't see that, then you deserve to lose everything that he is trying to give to you."

Alvin rolled back off of April and said, "Don't give me all that God's plan bullshit, you know full well we are not supposed to be here in this fucking situation."

April said, "You know what? I am going to believe and have the strength for the both of us. But mark my words Alvin, please don't let this blessing pass you by, or you will end up dying a lonely man."

Alvin didn't know what to say after that. He just got up, put on his clothes and told April that he had to leave. As she walked him to the door, she grabbed him around the waist again and said softly, "I love you."

Alvin just looked at her and opened the door without saying a word and left. When Alvin got home he laid on his bed trying to decide how he was going to explain this situation to Monica. No matter how hard he tried to find a way to make the situation lighter than it was, he knew that by telling her about this situation, their relationship would be over. Alvin then came to the conclusion that it was best not to tell Monica at all.

When Sunday came, Alvin arrived at Monica's house. When he looked at her, he couldn't help but notice that she was just a darker version of April with a whole lot more class. Alvin tongued kissed her for a long time, as if he hadn't seen her for days. "Wow Alvin, what did I do to deserve such a lovely greeting?"

Alvin started grinning "Because I really missed you and I wanted you to know that immediately when you opened up the door."

Monica pulled Alvin into the house and leaned him on the door. "I could really get used to coming home to this every day, you treating me like the true princess that I am."

"Well that you are my lovely dovely. You will always be treated like royalty by me."

They both went and sat on the couch. Monica didn't waste any time with her questions. "So what did you do all day yesterday dear? You didn't even call me."

Without hesitation, Alvin said, "Well I was actually working on a surprise for you. I can't really tell you what it is right now, but don't worry I will tell you soon."

"Really dear?" Monica said excitedly.

Alvin said, "You know what dear, every time I see you, you look more beautiful than the last time I saw you."

Monica put her arms around Alvin's neck and gave him a long seductive kiss on the lips. Alvin responded by putting his hands up Monica dress. Monica said, "Oh Alvin not here. You know I am going to wet up the couch."

Monica stood up and led Alvin to the bedroom. She pushed Alvin onto the bed and started taking off his shoes and then his pants. Alvin just laid there assisting whenever he could to help her undress him. Monica didn't even bother taking off her dress. She just reached under it and took off her bra. Monica slowly climbed up on Alvin and placed his cock inside of her. Alvin was so excited he started thrusting with force inside of her.

Monica put her hands up under Alvin's shirt without taking it off and started scratching him with both hands, from his shoulder blades all the way to his ribs. Alvin started to moan as she dug deeper into his skin. Alvin gazed passingly into Monica's Eyes and said, "I'm going to make an army of kids with you."

Monica, excited by his words, climaxed hard all over Alvin. She started screaming, "I can't make it stop, I can't make it stop!" Then she climaxed all over Alvin again.

At that point Alvin flipped her over and put her in a doggy style position. Alvin started pounding her from the back saying, "I don't want to ever lose this pussy. This pussy will always be mine." Before he could say another word, Monica climaxed again and collapsed on the bed. Alvin was still inside of her and he continued to go at it until he couldn't take it anymore and started cumming very hard inside of Monica. He rolled off of her and laid down beside her.

"Alvin, that was the best love making we ever had. I don't know what you were trying to prove, you already had me whipped the first time we made love."

Alvin whispered in an exhausted voice, "I meant every word that I said. You mean so much to me that I can't wait until we are one."

Monica rubbed her hands on Alvin's chest and felt the deep scratches that she put on him. "Baby I'm sorry, did I hurt you?"

Alvin placed his hand on top of hers and moved it up and down his chest. "No! I love it when you are aggressive like that. It felt so incredible that you turned me on more that I have ever been before. I couldn't help but want to please you.

Monica eyes widen as she placed a big grin on her face, "That's good to know. Whenever I want you to do it to me like that again, I would definitely know what to do."

Alvin inhaled a deep breath and moaned out, "Yes baby, you can do whatever you want to me. I am, and forever always, will be yours."

Monica leaned over and gave Alvin a kiss on the lips. She then pressed her body up against his and before you knew it, both of them were asleep. Later on that night, Alvin somehow got up the energy to make love to Monica again. When morning came, they both got up and went to work. When they reached the office, Joseph was standing outside and was shocked to see that they were walking arm in arm.

Once Alvin and Joseph were in the office together, Joseph asked Alvin what had happened over the weekend. Alvin with a disappointed look on his face said, "Not here bro. We can go for lunch later and I'll tell you then."

About an hour later Keisha called and asked Alvin the same question. He told her that it didn't go as planned and that he will explain everything in detail to her later on during the day.

With hesitation Keisha said, "Why do I get the feeling that you didn't do what you were supposed to do Alvin?"

"Don't worry Keisha. I will explain everything to you later." They both hung up and Alvin went back to doing his work.

When lunch time came, Alvin and Joseph went to lunch where Alvin started to explain to him what happened.

"Joe, let me tell you, I went to April's house thinking that I had everything under control. As soon as I walked into the door, it was like my whole plans just fell apart."

"Oh boy! what happened?" said, Joseph.

"Man, I really don't know what the hell happened. I walked in and asked her if she wanted to take the test now or later, she said she wanted to take it now. It's like the moment she retook that test and it came back positive, I became a different person," Alvin said while shaking his head.

"So how do you feel now that you know she could be having your kid?"

"It became a reality to me that for the first time in my life, I am actually going to be a father," Alvin said, placing his forehead in his cuffed hands. "What really bothers me about the whole thing is the sad fact that I had sex with her right after finding out. It felt like while I was inside of her; I was trying to get her pregnant all over again!"

Joseph shook his head in disbelief and said, "You have got to be out of your freaking mind! After everything that I told you, how could you go and do something so stupid? I bet you didn't even tell Monica about the situation, right?"

Alvin looked toward the ceiling and said in a low, soft voice, "No man, I couldn't do it. It's like when I'm with Monica, just being in her presence makes me feel like we are so right for each other. I really don't want to give all of that up."

Joseph replied, "But when you think of the reality of the situation, you are actually living a lie right now my brother. Believe me, it will come back to haunt in so many ways, that you are going to wish that you were dead just to escape the torment and torture."

"Man, I know I messed up. I really can't think right now because April is really trying to be with me. She laid some real grief shit on my conscience. It's like now when I think about her and all she is doing to try to turn her life around, I'm starting to have feelings for her that I thought I could never have."

Joseph stood up with disgust and paid the check, "I really feel sorry for you right now. No, I take that back. I actually feel sorrier for those two ladies that you're stringing along because you can't make up your mind about what the hell you want. If you ask me, I think you better get it together real fast, because right now, time is ticking and you are running out of options."

Alvin also got up and reached out to shake Joseph hands, "Yes, I know. Don't worry, I am going to try and figure something out."

Later that night when Alvin reached home, he dreaded calling Keisha because he knew she was going to say the same things that Joseph said. He took a shower and relaxed for a couple of hours. He decided to go ahead and call her anyway just because he had promised her he would.

When Keisha answered the phone, she said in a loud tone, "Alvin! I am so mad at you right now. Tell me what happened!"

Alvin cleared his throat and took a deep breath, "What can I say, I chickened out. I went to April's house and she took the test in front of me. It came up positive. Now I have to worry about becoming a father in a few months."

"Oh my God, how many months is she, because I know that I am going on three?"

"Well she was pregnant just a few weeks before you, so maybe about four months, or probably five considering when we had sex."

"So what happen on Sunday? Did you at least tell Monica what is going on?" Keisha asked.

"No. I couldn't do it. It was very hard for me to lose her the first time and I really don't want that to happen again. You have to understand that I really love this woman. I don't know how I'm going to break the news to her. I probably won't tell her at all."

"Alvin you are so playing with fire right now. I still say tell Monica the truth and deal with it. She forgave you once; If her love is truly real; she will find it in her heart to forgive you again."

"I don't know if I can do that Keisha!" Alvin snapped. "I mean it all sounds good, but the way I feel for Monica isn't going to let me take that risk again. Right now I am all confused because deep down, knowing that I am about to have my first child is messing with my head. I think I am starting to have feelings for April as well."

Keisha lost control and yelled, "What! Are you crazy? Oh my God Alvin, you are so messed up in the head right now. I am so disappointed in you. You were the most together guy I knew. I would tell everyone how I dated this guy who had his shit together. Now you are making me feel like you are becoming just a *typical asshole guy.*"

Alvin feeling both hurt and angry replied, "Listen, I know this situation is fucked up right now. The last thing I need right now is more negativity or for you to remind me how I'm messing up things. Trust me I get it. I'm an asshole!"

For a few seconds there was silence on the phone. In a sympathetic voice Keisha replied, "I'm sorry Alvin. Please forgive me for being insensitive to what you are going through and how you feel. As a woman being pregnant, I can understand what April is going through right now. As a woman who is engaged to be married to an awesome guy, I know exactly how Monica feels. As your friend, I am going to try to help you figure out what you should do. Again, please accept my apology Alvin for not listening to you objectively.

"Well I really appreciate you for at least trying to understand how I feel. I will listen to any advice you may have to offer."

"Okay, that's a start. Tell me how you really feel about April."

"At first I could care less for her because to me she was like a cheap fuck that I had sex with just because I was hurting for Monica. When I think about the way she changed her life just to please me and raise our child, I started to look at her in a different light."

"When I had sex with her on Saturday, I felt like it started out as pure lust because she was looking sexy as hell. Then all of a sudden, it was like I wanted to make love to her because she was carrying a part of me inside of her. I started believing in what she was saying about us being a family. It was at that moment I knew that I was starting to fall in love with her."

Keisha said, "I'm not even going to trip about you telling me that you two just had sex again. But I would say that was deep what you just said. So tell me, how do you really feel about Monica?"

"She is my angel. There isn't anything I wouldn't do for her. My heart is full and beats strong every time we are together. If there were really such a thing as 'soul mates', then that would be the most fitting words to describe her."

Keisha replied, "Gee Alvin, I don't even know where to begin on this one. But I will tell you this. Somebody is going to have to lose. You are going to have to figure out who it's going to be. I'm sorry to say this, but you can't have them both. In my opinion even if Monica forgives you, if you two get married she will find it hard to trust you. When it's time for you to go over to April's house and see your kid, I'm sure she'll be highly upset on many occasions. So you might want to think very hard about that.

On the other hand, you have April. You are starting to have feelings for her, which is great. If you were to choose her, at least you could build on something that could become very real for the both of you. Plus, when you add in the kid, you will still have that family that you always wanted. The only downside that I see with you being with her is, you would kind of secretly hate April because deep down you rather would want to be with Monica instead of her. In other words, you would feel like you have settled for less. So there you have my opinion. I can't tell you who to choose, that choice will have to be up to you."

"Thank you for your honest opinion. Don't worry, I heard every word that you said and I know now what I have to do. To be honest if I had to choose today I would choose April. What you said about Monica trusting me seems very logical to me. Besides, I love her enough to want her to be with someone who is going to give her a clean slate without any drama. So I guess I am going to have to give up the thought of us ever being together."

Keisha gasped "Wow! I never thought in a million years you would say that. That actually took me for a little loop. But, it's your decision and I am glad that you came to terms with the situation. My only question to you now is; When are you going to tell Monica?"

"I assure you Keisha, before the end of the week, she will know everything."

"I do hope so Alvin. And this time, please don't punk out. I love you too much and I really don't want to see anything bad happening with you."

Alvin replied, "In some weird type of way, I love you too and thank you very much for being a friend when I needed one."

"Ah that's alright bighead. I will talk to you soon."

Chapter Nine

Problems Mounting

They both hung up the phone. Alvin felt really good after talking to Keisha. He laid down for a few minutes and then picked up the phone again to call Monica. When Monica answered, Alvin said, "Hey baby, how are you doing tonight?"

"Oh Alvin my love. I am doing much better now that I am hearing your voice."

"Oh stop that. Did I wake you?"

"No, I haven't been feeling well lately. But it would be nice if you could come over and keep me company."

"I thought about it, but it's getting kind of late and we both have to get up early in the morning. I was just calling to make sure that you are alright,"

"Well like I told you, I haven't been feeling too well. I don't think that I will be going in tomorrow. I will probably see if I could get an appointment with my doctor."

"Aw baby I'm really sorry to hear that," Alvin cooed. "If you like I will take off and come with you."

"No baby, it wouldn't look good if we both took off. Besides, I really don't think it will be that big of a deal. It's probably something I've ate.

They talked for a little while longer and then went to bed. The next day, Alvin called April while he was at work. April picked up and said, "Hello my future baby daddy. I was just thinking about how good you were fucking me the other day. I am so horny and wet right now."

Alvin sigh "I have to admit, I really enjoyed being inside of you, but that isn't the reason why I called. If you have time later I would like to come over and talk to you."

"You know I will always have time for you honey," April said softly. "I would be more than happy to see you again. I might just have a surprise for you when you come over."

Alvin said, "No, I really don't want any surprises. All I want to do is just talk, that's it."

"Okay baby, we will see what happens when you come over. And Alvin, I love you! See there I said it."

Alvin's reaction was cold, he only responded by saying, "I will see you later," and he hung up the phone.

Later that afternoon, just before Alvin was about to get ready to go home; Monica walked into his office.

"Hi baby", Monica said with a big smile on her face. "

I just wanted to stop by before you go home to tell you how my day went at the doctor's office. I'm afraid I have bad news to tell you."

Alvin face became flush, because in his mind, He was hoping that he didn't catch anything from April. "Oh? I hope it isn't too bad. I really wouldn't want anything happening to you."

Monica stared deeply into Alvin's eyes and said, "Are you seeing anyone else? The reason why I am asking is because you gave me something."

"No!" Alvin said loudly. "Are you sure it was me? I don't have anything wrong with me."

Monica now looking at Alvin with disappointment said, "What are you trying to say, do you think I was cheating on you? How dare you say that to me Alvin."

"Well babe when you asked me a question like that, of course I was going to be on the defensive side."

Monica continued to stare Alvin in the eyes and busted out laughing. "Look, if you didn't give it to me I don't know how else I got it. So I am pretty sure it was you who gave it to me."

"Why don't you just tell me what you have?" Alvin said with a grin on his face now that he sees her laughing and smiling.

"I am pregnant." Monica yelled out.

Alvin filled with excitement walked over to her and gave her a big hug and kiss. "Oh my God, you mean to tell me that I am about to be a father?"

"Yes!" Monica replied. I was so excited when I heard the news, I just had to come right over and tell you. My darling, besides the time that you proposed to me, this has got to be the greatest moment in my entire life. I'm treating you out to dinner tonight to celebrate. Anything you want, you can have, because you are my king!"

"Well I am kind of tired. Would you like to do this another time?"

"Babe I know you had a hard day, but it would mean a lot to me if we could sit down and talk over dinner tonight. There is so many thoughts and emotions that are going through my mind right now; I just want to share them all with you."

Alvin hugged Monica again with passion and said, "Okay baby, I am all yours."

They left and went out to dinner. Before going home after they ate dinner, Alvin went to the bathroom and checked his phone because he had it off the whole time. He saw that April was calling and texting him all night. He sent her a text telling her that something came up and he wasn't able to make it. April immediately texted him back saying, *"I know that fucking bitch Monica came up Alvin. I don't like it when you keep choosing her over me, especially after you already made plans with me!"*

Alvin texted back, "Sorry", and turned off his phone again. When Alvin went back out, he told Monica that he wanted to go back home with her. In his mind he didn't know if April was going to show up at his place or not. Monica agreed and they both left.

The next day they both got to work and again they were arm-in-arm. Monica was beaming and couldn't wait to tell her friends and coworker the good news. Monica and Alvin kissed and then went their separate ways. When Alvin got to his office, he went over to Joseph and whispered, "Man you are not going to believe this shit."

Joseph's eyes widened and he said, "What happened?"

"Just when you think that things can't get any worse, it does. I just found out that Monica is pregnant."

"Man, I was trying to tell you that you can't run and hide from your mistakes. At some point you are going to have to face the problem for what it is or the problem will find a way to reveal itself."

Alvin hung his head down, "For some reason I just can't get ahead of what's happening. Every time I think I have it all figured out and plan my move, it seems like something keeps pulling me away from exposing the real truth."

"Hey, I don't want to sound like a bastard or anything, but you are the problem Alvin. Instead of just letting everyone know what's going on, you are trying to figure out ways to sugar coat everything. If you ask me, you are going to lose both of those women and your kids if you keep this up."

Alvin's heart felt heavy, "Yes I know what you mean. I was supposed to meet up with April last night but I stood her up. I know that she is very pissed off right now. I didn't even want to go home last night, because I was afraid that she would have shown up while Monica and I were there."

Joseph shook his head and said, "At this point my brother, I really don't have anything else to say. All I can do is wish you the best of luck."

Joseph patted Alvin on the back and went to his desk. Alvin followed right behind him and said, "Hey Joe, I need you to take over and cover for me today. I really can't be here right now. I have too much stuff going on in my head. I could really use a break and I know that I wouldn't be able to concentrate while I am here anyway."

Joseph replied, "No problem boss. Go and do what you have to do and take as long as you want. I got this."

"Thanks man, you have been more help to me than you can imagine. I will not forget all you have done for me," said, Alvin.

Joseph smiled and replied, "Forget that, I better get a good bonus check at the end of the year!"

Alvin grinned and while walking out the door he said, "That's all you want? Okay, then I will forget about that raise I was going to give you."

Alvin left the office and started walking aimlessly down the street. The whole time he was thinking about how he was going to make things right. He thought about going to April's house, but he quickly decided against that decision. He wanted to call Keisha, but he really didn't feel like talking to anyone. He thought to himself that this was something that he had to figure out all on his own.

As he was walking, he came across a school yard where preschoolers were playing outside. He stopped and looked at them while they were playing. In his mind he was thinking about how nice it would be to be one of those father bringing his kids to the park. As he stood there and continued to watch, a tear began to roll down his face. Having two kids on the way from two different women, he realized that they might never be able to play together.

Alvin wiped his tear away and started walking again. He started thinking to himself. *What if I just go and see a psychologist? Maybe by talking about it to someone who doesn't know me, I can get a different opinion on what to do.* He quickly rejected the idea because he knew what Joseph said was true. At some point, he is going to have to just tell both women what is going on and deal head on with the consequences.

Alvin grew tired of walking and decided that he needed a drink to clear his head and help him forget about his problems for a little while, so he headed to a sport bar that was close by. When he reached there,

Alvin saw that the place was pretty much empty because it was still fairly early. As he walked up to the bar and sat down, he noticed that there was a young white woman sitting at the bar talking to the bartender. She looked as though she was very upset about something.

Alvin didn't want to sit too close to her because all he wanted to do was just have his drink and leave. As soon as he sat down the woman and the bartender started staring at him. Alvin nodded and then turned to stare at the big television that sat in the middle of the bar. The woman, whose face was still flushed, started to smile and got up. She walked toward Alvin and said, "Excuse me sir, I could really use someone to talk to right now; and since you are the only one here and have a kind face, I was wondering if you could have a drink with me and talk?"

Alvin slowly shook his head no and said, "I'm sorry but I have so much going on right now, I really don't think I can help you. Besides, wasn't you talking to the bartender?"

The young woman gave a rejected smiled and tears started rolling down her face. She said, "That's okay, I'm sorry to have bothered you," and started walking away.

Alvin feeling bad said, "Stop! Sit down and tell me why you are so upset." The young woman said, "It's okay, you don't have to worry about me, I will be fine." She continued to walk away.

Alvin got up, grabbed her hands and led her back to a seat next to him at the bar.

"I am sorry for being so rude, just talk to me and tell me what's troubling you."

The young woman dried her face. "Thank you. First I will tell you that my name is Judith, but you could call me Judy."

"Very nice to meet you Judy." Alvin said as he reaches out to shake her hands. "You can call me Alvin."

"Hi Alvin, nice to meet you as well." Judy dried all of the tears away from her face and began telling Alvin her story.

"Okay, I don't know where to start so I guess I will start from the beginning. A few days ago my boyfriend and I were coming home from having dinner when a couple of guys stopped us. My boyfriend looks almost just like you. That was the reason why I was staring so hard at you as you walked in."

Alvin interrupted, "So are you telling me that you were dating a black guy?"

"Yes." Replied Judy. "Anyway they started to call us names but we just kept on walking. I pulled out my cell phone and told them that I was going to call the police if they didn't leave us alone. That was when one of the guys slapped my hands and my phone felled to the ground. My boyfriend was already upset but he didn't do anything until that happened. He turned around cursing out the two guys and told them that he's going to kick their ass if they don't leave us alone.

"That is when one of the guys pushed him real hard and he fell to the ground. The other guy grabbed me and started feeling all over my breasts while laughing and taunting my boyfriend. My boyfriend got up and ran toward the guy who was holding me. But before he could reach me, the other guy pulled out a knife and stabbed him in his sides puncturing his lungs."

Judy started gasping for air as she began to cry hysterically. "I started screaming for help but it was too late. My boyfriend died while I was holding him in my arms. I loved him so much! Why did they have to kill him?"

Alvin stand up and put his arms around Judy. "I am really sorry that you had to go through that. Did they ever catch the guys that did it?"

Again Judy dried her eyes and said, "Yes they caught them that night. I had to go down to the precinct and identify them. I have an appointment to go see the prosecutor next week."

"Well that's good, I'm glad they caught them."

"Thanks, but the real reason why I am so upset is because my boyfriend's funeral is tomorrow and his family never did like me for dating him. They kind of like disowned him like my family disowned me. It seemed as though it was pretty much us against the world. I'm afraid that they blame me for his death. If I wasn't dating him, he probably would still be alive."

Alvin took both of Judy's hands and gave her a stern look into her eyes, "Listen! Sometimes things happen in life that we don't have any control over. I want you to please understand that you didn't have anything to do with your boyfriend's death. Those assholes were the real reason why he died that night. So I'm going to tell you to go to that funeral with your head up high, and pay your last respects to the man that you loved."

Judy now snuffling looked at Alvin with her eye's all teary and said, "You know I really wish it could be that easy. Deep down I do feel as though I am responsible. Of course I would like to see him one last time, but I know I will break down the moment I see him lying there in that coffin.

We lived together for three years and no one knows him like I do. He was everything to me and I can't face seeing him in that coffin."

"Well isn't there anyone that could go with you?" Alvin asked.

"No. All of my family is in Maine, and like I said before, it was pretty much just me and him. I didn't make any friends while we were living here."

Alvin hugged her again and said, "Well I know that we just met, but if you need someone to be there for support, I guess I can come with you."

"Really? You would do that for a complete stranger that you just met in a bar?" said, Judy as she looked up at him with tears in her eyes.

"Well what kind of world would we live in if people don't go out of their way to help a complete stranger?"

"Yes, you are right. When I first saw you, it felt like it was him who was pushing me over to talk to you. I could tell you were a nice guy the moment I saw you."

"Yes, but sometimes too nice to a fault," said Alvin, as he looked away for a brief moment.

"So how would you like to do this? Would you like for me to come and pick you up, or would you prefer for me to meet you there?"

"Well if you don't mind, I really would love for you to pick me up. I don't think I will be in any condition to drive there myself and back."

"Okay, just give me all of your information and the time you want me to come get you." Judy wrote down her information, and hugged Alvin very tight.

"Thank you so much, I know your wife is truly lucky to have a nice guy like you."

Alvin gently push her back and smiled., "Now do I look like the type of guy that would take off his wedding ring and come to a bar?"

Judy replied, "No I'm sorry, maybe I should have asked before I assumed you were married."

"That's okay, but I am engaged though."

"Well good for you. Bobby and I were saving up for a wedding, but it was like we never could save up enough. I know you said that you were having problems. What's going on with you?"

Alvin sigh as he quickly remembered the reason why he was there, "Well I guess we can talk about me another time. I'm going to have to go. Are you going to be alright?"

"That's fine Alvin. I believe you have given me new hope. I will be fine thank you. I guess I should be going as well. I have to find something to wear for tomorrow."

"Okay, that really sounds like a plan. By the way, did anyone ever tell you that you look a little like a younger version of Madonna?"

Judy eyes seems to sparkle as they widen, "Oh my God, that was the first thing Bobby said when he first walked over to me."

Alvin replied, "Well you do look a lot like her. It's almost scary actually."

"Well I don't know if that's a good thing or a bad thing, but thank you for putting a smile on my face. I didn't think I was going to be smiling anytime soon," said, Judy with a big wide grin.

They stood up, embraced and walked out. Alvin walked back to the office, but before he got there, he brought some flowers to give to Monica. Monica was still all bright-eyed when she saw him. Alvin handed her the flowers and she placed them under her nose to smell them. "For me! Thank you baby, now that's why I am always going to love you forever."

Alvin smiled and began telling Monica that he wouldn't be in tomorrow because he had to go to a friend's funeral. Monica sounded disappointed because she wanted to spend the night with Alvin. She didn't ask any questions about his friend either because she was still up in the clouds about her good news. When it was time for them to leave, they both went their separate ways.

When Alvin got home he wasted no time calling April. April answered the phone in a nasty loud tone, "You just now getting back to me motherfucker?"

Alvin moved the phone slightly from his ears, "Listen, are you going to let me explain what happened or are you going to just keep on cursing while I'm trying to talk to you?"

April replied, "I know damn well what happened, like always you choose to hurt my feelings and spare Monica. I am sure this isn't going to be the last time you do this shit Alvin."

While hearing April crying. Alvin said, "Listen, I really don't want to do this over the phone, can I come over?"

"You know I am not going to deny you from coming over here."

"Just to let you know, I am not staying over because I have a funeral to go to tomorrow," explained Alvin.

"That is fine with me. I have a doctor's appointment in the morning as well."

When Alvin reached April's house, she opened the door and stood there with arms extended out. "Don't you miss me a little Alvin? The least you could do is give me a hug or a kiss or something."

Alvin leaned over and pecked April on the forehead. April said, "Gee thanks a lot Alvin, you really know how to make a woman feel special."

"I just want to let you know what happened last night and then I have to go," said, Alvin.

They both went to sit on the sofa. April draped her legs on top of Alvin and said, "Okay, I am listening."

Before Alvin could talk, April wrapped her arm around his neck and placed her hand on his chest.

Alvin said, "How do you suppose we can have a serious conversation if you are trying to seduce me?"

"I'm not trying to seduce you. I am just appreciating your company while you are here. I said go ahead, I am listening."

Alvin put his hands on top of April's legs and started rubbing them. He looked into April's eyes and said, "The reason why I couldn't make it yesterday was because Monica came to my job yesterday and told me that she was pregnant."

April stayed silent for a moment. She then looked at Alvin and said, "Then I guess you are fucked huh. I mean, what can I say to that shit Alvin? I kind of knew that you were going to try and get her pregnant just because you didn't want to be with me. Am I correct?"

Alvin shook his head "I had no intention of getting her pregnant like that. The truth of the matter is; I am starting to really fall for you. Now with this situation blowing up in my face I really don't know what to do anymore."

April grabbed Alvin hand, placed it under her skirt and started rubbing her pussy with it. "Do you want to keep this Alvin? Because you know it belongs to you and only you," she said. She removed her hands, but Alvin kept rubbing on her pussy not saying a word. He then started fingering her until she started moaning and she eventually climaxed.

Alvin said, "I really don't know what it is about you. I mean, you are very beautiful. You can be civil when you want to be, and for some reason whenever I am around you, it's like I can't get enough of you. To be honest I don't know if it's actually lust or if I am genuinely falling in love with you."

April removed her legs from Alvin's lap and began unzipping his pants. "Hold that thought for a minute, I owe you one."

April reached into his pants and pulled out his cock. She started deep throating it slowly until Alvin couldn't hold it any longer and climaxed inside of her mouth. April held her head up, swallowed Alvin's cum and said, "You love me, because I am the only woman who knows how to give it to you anyway and everyway, and your mind and body will always crave for me. Tell me if I am lying or not. You know that I am right."

Alvin took a deep breath and said, "As much as I want to, I don't think I will ever be able to get you out of my system. So you are right, I am in love with you." April smiled and stood up, grabbed Alvin's hands, and led him to the bedroom where they made love into the wee hours of the morning.

Alvin woke up early enough to go home and take a shower. When he got dressed he called Judy to make sure that she was ready. As he pulled up to Judy's Apartment complex, he called and told her that he was outside. Judy in a very nervous voice said, "Alvin, I'm really sorry. I don't think I can do this."

"No. You are just having cold feet right now. I'm going to come up and get you."

"Okay, maybe I just need that extra push."

When Alvin reached Judy's apartment she opened up the door. Alvin was struck by how beautiful she looked in all black with makeup on.

"Wow! Is this the same woman that I met in the bar yesterday? You look absolutely beautiful!"

"Thank you Alvin, but do you think that I might have over done it?"

Alvin shook his head in disbelief. "Not at all. So come on, let's go say good bye to the man that you love."

Alvin held out his arm. Judy put her arm in his and they walked to the car. When they reached the funeral home Alvin said, "Okay Judy, from this point on, I want you to know that I have your back. If anyone gets out of line just let me do the talking for you."

Judy shook her head yes and agreed. As they walked in the seating area, heads immediately turned toward them. You could hear that people were starting to whisper. Halfway down the Aisle, Judy sat down where there were a few people already sitting.

But right at that moment as Alvin began to sit down beside her, Bobby's mother Ms. Elaine came over and said, "No dear, you are family now. Come and sit up front with the rest of us where you belong."

Alvin smiled at Judy and said, "You go ahead. I will stay here."

Judy looked shocked but got up and went to the front with Ms. Elaine.

The funeral lasted for about two hours. There were lots of songs and the preacher even preached a great sermon. The best part was when Judy got up to testify about how much she loved Bobby, and said that she was very grateful that the family accepted her being there.

When the service was over, Judy walked over to Alvin and said, "Thank you very much for giving me the courage to come here. The family asked me to ride with them in the limo to the burial. I just wanted to make sure that it would be alright with you."

"I am very proud of the way that you handled yourself. I want you to go ahead with them and bond with the family. I'm sure you have a lot of stories about Bobby that they would want to hear. I'm going to go home and get some much needed rest.

Judy smiled and embraced Alvin. She placed a kissed on his chin and said, "I am in your debt. If ever you need anything, please let me know. More importantly, I hope that we can become and remain good friends.

Alvin looked into Judy's eyes and said, "Sometimes God brings people together for a reason. I am very happy that I met you. Yes, I can see us being good friends. Now go and be with your new family."

Alvin Hugged Judy one last time as he headed toward his car. Once he got inside, he called Monica to let her know that the services were over and that he was coming over. When he got there, Monica opened up the door and gave him a big hug.

"Wow, are you trying to tell me that you missed me?"

"Yes, I was thinking about you all day. How did it go at your friend's funeral today?"

"It was very sad, but it was better than most funerals that I've been to. But let's not talk about that, how was your day mommy?"

"It was okay. The baby had me sleeping all morning. I was too tired to do anything else. But I was thinking Alvin; don't you think we should get married way before the baby comes? I really would want to be able to walk around and stand up."

"Yes I thought about that. When would you like to get married?"

"As soon as possible. Monica quickly replied. "You do know that I am already two months."

"Wow it's been two months already? Time is really flying by. Okay babe, how about next month we just go ahead and get married and have the ceremony a little later after the baby is born?"

Monica pulled Alvin closer to her and gave him a big hug and kiss. Monica rested her head on Alvin chest and whispered, "I love you so much Alvin. You have made me the happiest woman in the whole wide world."

Chapter Ten

The Face Off

Alvin spent the whole weekend over at Monica's house. That Monday they both got up and went to work together. While at work April called Alvin and said, "Where have you been Alvin? I didn't hear from you the whole weekend. Is everything alright?"

Alvin took a deep breath and said, "Well after the funeral I went over to Monica house and spent the weekend over there."

"I'm not even going to trip. Do you know that I have only five more months before I have your child Alvin? When are you going to start taking responsibility for your feelings about who you want to be with?

"Listen, now isn't the best time to talk about this. I'll call you when I get home."

"No you listen, either we talk about this now or I'm coming to your job and we all can talk about it together. I'm really getting tired of this shit Alvin. I deserve more than that."

Alvin got angry and said, "Don't you come down here and bring drama to my job. If you don't want me to lose all respect for you, that will be the last thing you want to do."

"Respect! You keep throwing Monica up in my face and you talk about respect?"

Alvin drew in a deep breath and angrily said, "Again, I don't want to talk about this right now. I'll give you a call when I get home!"

Alvin didn't wait for a response from April and hung up the phone. As the work day was coming to an end, Mr. Charles came to Alvin's office and with a stern but disappointed voice said, "Alvin, April was in the lobby looking for you and talking a lot of shit, asking where Monica is. I took her to my office to calm her down, but you better get in there and handle that situation."

Alvin was filled with rage. You could see the fire in his eyes as they began to turn red, "That mother fucking bitch! Do you know where Monica is?"

"I guess she is in her office."

"Okay let me go talk to this bitch and get her out of here." Alvin went to Mr. Charles' office and saw April sitting in his seat behind the desk.

April with a very devilish look on her face, put up her right hands as to say stop and said, "Before you even open your mouth to say anything, you better listen up very carefully. Don't you ever disrespect me again and hang the phone up on me. I am not someone you can play childish games with Alvin. I have feelings too, and being pregnant right now with your child, I am one hell of a stressed out cranky bitch!"

Before Alvin was able to utter a word, someone knocked on the door. Alvin didn't say anything, but Monica opened up the door and saw April sitting behind Mr. Charles' desk.

Monica looking both surprised and worried said, "Alvin what is going on here?"

April without even giving Alvin a chance to speak blurted out, "You must be Ms. Monica. Alvin was right, we pretty much could pass for sisters. By the way, I am April. It's so nice to finally meet you. Now go ahead Alvin, why don't you tell her what's going on?"

Alvin grabbed Monica by the hands and tried to lead her through the door. Alvin looking both nervous and frighten said, "Don't worry I will explain everything to you later."

Monica violently pushed him off and said, "No! I want you to explain it now. What the hell is going on here Alvin?"

April, who started smiling and laughing hectically said in a patronizing tone "Oh I like her."

Alvin turned to April and in a loud voice said, "April, why don't you just shut the fuck up and get out."

The smile on April's face quickly evaporated and she stood up and said, "Fuck you! This is my show and I am about to be heard up in this bitch today."

Monica was both heartbroken and stung when she looked at April and saw that she was pregnant. She walked out of the office covering her face crying. Alvin called out to her but he didn't go after her.

He just gave a nasty look of disgust at April and said, "I never want to see you again. Fuck you and that baby!"

Alvin walked out of Mr. Charles office not caring whatever April had to say and went to look for Monica. He never was able to find her. Days turned into weeks. Alvin would call and go by Monica's house and he would never get a reply back. Monica never showed up to work or even called to let Mr. Charles know if she was even coming back.

A few days later Alvin went to the precinct to file a missing person report. He wanted to see if the police would be able to at least let him know that she was alright. Within a day while Alvin was at home, he received a phone call from a detective Johnson telling him that they found Monica dead in her home. The detective went on to say that it looked like a suicide, because she left him a note. "We would also like for you to come down to the morgue and identify her body." The detective said. Alvin agreed and hung up the phone.

He sat on his bed for a moment and then it hit him. While rocking back and forth, he placed his hands on top of his head and started crying hysterically, "Oh my God what have I done? My Monica is dead. My Monica is dead!" He wept all through the night. In the morning he called Keisha and told her the news.

Keisha heart seems to pound heavy in her chest, "Oh my God Alvin, I am so sorry to hear that. You have my condolences." You can tell in Keisha's voice that she was going to start crying.

Alvin while talking to Keisha, tried to remain calm and strong, "I am so numb inside right now I don't know what I'm supposed to do. I have to go down later to identify her body. I just don't know if I can see her lying there dead with my baby inside of her."

"If you like Alvin, I can go with you."

"Thanks Keisha, but I know this is something I have to do alone."

"Well you know I will always be there for you Alvin, no matter what. I love you."

"Thank you Keisha. I really appreciate that. I love you too."

Alvin hung up and immediately his phone rang. It was April. He didn't answer the phone, he just let it go to his voicemail. After the call was finished, he listened to it.

It was hard for him to hear the message because April was crying and mumbling her words, *"Alvin I was watching the news and they said they found a pregnant woman's body named Monica in her home. Please call me and tell me that wasn't her. If so, I am so ashamed of myself right now. Please Alvin, call me, I have to know!"*

Alvin just shook his head and got dressed and went to the morgue. There detective Jones ask him a few questions. Before he took him to go and see her body, he also showed Alvin the suicide note that was going to be put into evidence. It read:

Dear Alvin,

As I lay here crying over the dim future that you have placed before us, I can't help but think about all the things that have happened to me in my life. Everyone seems to die around me. No matter how hard I try to find happiness, it would appear that happiness is the last thing God wanted me to have.

When I gave you another chance, I trusted you with my life, and believed that you and the baby were going to be my new beginning. My light was shining as bright as a star knowing that we were going to be a family forever, and in an instant, you distinguished my flame. Words cannot express the hurt and pain that you have inflicted upon me.

So I want you to feel that pain the way that I do. That pain of losing something much greater than you. I will take our child to heaven with me and hopefully God will be able to see my heart and forgive me for not only taking my life, but our child's as well.

I love you very much Alvin, but you will never be able to have me now. You will never be able to have us! I'm sorry your love wasn't strong enough for the both of us!

Monica

Alvin gave the note back to detective Jones and went into a corner, covering his eyes and crying.

"I'm sorry I don't think I can do this." Alvin muffled

Detective Jones placed his hands on Alvin's back and said, "It's okay, right now I just want you to be strong and we can get through this. I will give you a few minutes for you to compose yourself and then you let me know when you are ready."

Alvin nodded his head and said "Okay."

After a few minutes, Alvin was ready. Detective Jones led Alvin to a big empty room with only a chair and small desk. "We don't show the actual body anymore, so what I want you to do is look at these photos and just say yes if it's her. However, I do have to warn you, she might not look the way you remember her. So please take your time and make absolutely sure that this is her."

Detective Jones gave Alvin the photos and Alvin could hardly look at them because her body was so badly decomposed. Then Alvin looked deeper behind all the gore, and he knew that this was the woman that he deeply loved.

Alvin felt a lump growing inside of his throat. With his eyes starting to tear up again he said, "Yes, That's her. I am positively sure that it is her."

"Thank you, we will be in touch to let you know when we will be able to release her body for burial."

Alvin shook detective Jones' hands and left. Before Alvin left the building, he found an empty bench and sat there quietly for a few moments. The Phone rang and he saw that it was Judy calling him.

Alvin answered the phone and Judy said, "Hello Alvin, I haven't heard from you since the funeral. Is everything okay? I wanted to tell you what happened later on that day."

Alvin still in shock after seeing the horrifying pictures of Monica cleared his throat and said, "Hello Judy, I wish I could talk right now, but I am at the morgue. I had to come down here to identify my fiancée."

Judy didn't waste any time consulting him, "Oh my God Alvin, I'm so sorry to hear that. That's horrible! Please tell me what happened to her?"

"I wish I could talk about it right now, but I really can't. I will give you a call later once I clear my head."

"That's okay Alvin. You take as much time as you need. Again I am so sorry to hear about your lost. Please call me back later. I really want to be there for you like you were for me. Promise me Alvin."

"I promise you whenever I need someone to help me get through this, you will be the first person that I call. Good bye."

They hung up the phone, and he got up and went to his car and drove home. Once Alvin reached home, he didn't know how to feel. On the one hand, he just wanted to be alone and not talk to anyone. On the other hand, he felt as though he needed a lot of people around him. Just so that he could take his mind off all the things he wished he would had done differently. He looked at the messages on his phone from April and all he could think about was *I wish it was her instead.*

The more he thought about it, the more Alvin wanted to call April. He just didn't have the words to say to her. Instead, Alvin called Mr. Charles at the office and told him how everything went at the morgue.

Mr. Charles said, "I know you are hurting right now Alvin. I want you to take as much time as you like so that you can get you head right. I don't want you to go and do something that you regret. I really know how much you loved Monica. We all did."

"When I think about coming back to work, all I want to do is see her face when I get there," Said Alvin. "I have never felt this way ever in my life. In her note, she wrote that she wanted me to feel like she did. Boss man, I have to tell you, I feel exactly the way she did right now. If I had half the courage that she had, I would take my life as well."

"Now hold on my friend, Mr. Charles said with worry in his voice. "I know that pain you are feeling right now is more than any man could ever bear, but what I want you to start thinking about is giving Monica and your baby a decent homecoming. You don't even have to worry about the expense of the funereal. The company will pay for everything."

"Yes you are right. You don't have to worry, because like I said, I'm not half as brave as she was. I will let you know when they release her body."

"Okay Alvin, I'm happy to hear that. I need you to stay strong for all of us. If ever you need anything just give me a call. It could be anytime, day or night, I am here for you Alvin."

"Thank you sir. Don't worry, if I need anything I will call you. Good bye."

Alvin got up, took a shower and began to get dressed. When he was done, he gave Joseph a call.

"Hello Joseph, I'm sure you already heard about Monica."

"Yes, I am still hurting about all of that. I guess I can only imagine what you are going through."

"Trust me, right now it like I am constantly having this out-of-body experiences. That's the reason why I am calling you. I wanted to know if you would like to hang out with me. I need to get a few drinks into my system and get out of this house."

"Well the getting out of the house part is definitely a good ideal," said, Joseph. "I'm not so sure about the drinking part. But to be honest with you, as much as I would like to go with you tonight I can't. Remember when I was telling you about my son that I didn't know the whereabouts of?"

"Yes I remember."

"Well I got a letter a few weeks ago from a young man who says he thinks that I am his father. He left his number and I called him. It turns out that he is actually indeed my son. I was going to pick him up at the airport in a few minutes and bring him back home to my place."

"Wow, that is very beautiful. That's the kind of news that I needed to hear, something positive. I am very happy for the both of you."

"Thanks man. I tell you, sometimes God can work in mysterious ways. That's why I hope you can understand that what happened to Monica isn't your fault. All the things that were set into motion were all of God's plans to work out the situation and bring his angels home. I know that you are mad at April right now, but you need to learn to forgive her and try to make the best of this situation."

"I don't even want to talk about April right now. You're right, it's going to take a lot of drinks in my system to even think about forgiving her for what she's done."

"See that's where you are wrong," said, Joseph. "Just as I told you it wasn't your fault, you have to take that blame away from her as well and learn to move on. I know it's going to take a little bit of time, but just listen and let time heal all your wounds."

"Yes, I hear you. I will try anything at this point. I really don't have anything else to lose."

"No, you could lose a whole lot more. I just want you to think smart right now and don't let the pain drive you to do something you might regret later on. Remember, I've kind of been where you are right now. I understand fully what you are going through. Just be smart and stay safe."

"I always appreciate your wisdom and insight on things," said, Alvin. "So don't worry, I will do my best to try and follow your advice. I do hope that everything goes well with your son. I will catch up with you later to let you know when and where and when Monica's funeral is going to be."

"Thanks Alvin, I will be there. Of course if you need anything, anything at all, I am here for you."

"Thank you, I will remember that. I'll talk to you later."

They both hung up, and since he was already dressed Alvin knew that he was still going to go out, but he didn't know where. He then picked up his phone and called Judy.

"Hello Judy, I was wondering if you were free to go and have a few drinks with me tonight?"

"Sure Alvin. I was just sitting here thinking I needed to get out this house, but I didn't know what to do with myself. I am very glad that you called. Are you okay though?"

"I'm trying real hard to be Judy. I just want to unwind and try to forget about a few things right now. I guess I could also use the company. Plus, I could use any experience you have with how to plan a funeral."

"Say no more," said, Judy. "I have a great idea. Why don't you meet me at the sport bar where we met?"

"Okay, I hadn't thought about that place. That would be perfect. What time would you like to meet?"

"I am already dressed, so whatever time you say, I will be there."

"I'll leave right now and see you when you get there," said, Alvin.

Judy said, "Remember I live just a few blocks away so I will probably get there before you. But in any case it really doesn't matter. I'll just see you there."

Alvin agreed and they both hung up the phone. When Alvin got into his car, his phone rang again. It was April. Again, he didn't answer the phone and let the call go straight to his voice mail. Afterwards he listened to the message.

"Alvin, I know it was Monica that killed herself. When you said you didn't want to have anything to do with me and our baby, you hurt me deeply that day in the office. I haven't stopped crying since I heard the news because I know what you said that day will be even more true now. If I could take back everything that I did that day I would."

She began to cry. *"I don't care if you don't ever want anything to do with me again. But please Alvin, the baby is innocent. She's going need her father in her life. I will do whatever it takes to make sure you two have a great relationship. Just find it in your heart not to punish her for my wrong doing. Of course I only did what I did that day because I am so deeply in love with you and was very jealous of the close relationship you had with Monica over me. I would do anything to have you in my life, Alvin. But I will leave that up to you. Just give me a call and talk to me. I love you Alvin, always."*

Chapter Eleven

The Funeral

Alvin sat in his car and started to cry, but he held back his tears. On one hand he wanted to do what Joseph said and try to forgive her, but then when he thought about that day in the office, only his rage would surface.

Alvin got himself together and went to the sport bar. When he got there, he saw Judy sitting in that same spot where they first started talking.

Judy Got up and gave Alvin a big hug and said, "See I told you I was going to beat you here. I already ordered the first round!"

Alvin said "Okay, thank you. It's nice to see you. Why you came here all sexy like that? This wasn't a date."

"I dressed up like this to take your mind off of everything that you are going through right now. I wanted you to focus on me and what I have to say to you."

Alvin laughed and said, "Trust me, you didn't have to dress up like that to get my attention, but I appreciate the gesture."

"Oh Alvin, now you're making me feel bad. I can go home and change and come back if you like?"

"No that's okay," said Alvin, giggling to himself. "As you can see you already brought a smile to my face so I guess that's a good thing. I didn't think I was going to be able to ever smile again."

"See that's exactly what you did for me. So I am glad that I could do the same for you.

"Who could ever imagine that somehow we are meant to support each other, and that it was fate which brought us into each other's lives," Alvin replied

Well I'm not going to pressure you to talk about your situation. I know that this has been really hard on you. So we can talk about anything that you may like." Said Judy.

Alvin reached for his glass, "How about I get some of this alcohol into my system first and you tell me what happened after we left the funeral that day."

Judy's eyes widen and she started to smile. "Oh yeah, let me tell you Alvin. While we were riding in the limo, Bobby's mother put her arms around me and started telling her kids that from now on they are to treat me as a member of this family. All these years that she was with Bobby, we should have done that a long time ago.

"So everyone in the limo started crying and hugging me. I'm all in tears. When we get to the burial site, everyone started saying their last words. Bobby's mother then gave me a white rose and said she wanted me to be the first one to place it on his casket. Alvin let me tell you, I was on such an emotional high that day I didn't know what to do with myself. Afterward, we went to his mother's house and if you want to talk about eating, I haven't eaten like that on all my Thanksgivings put together. His family knows how to throw down in the kitchen!

"Later, we all exchanged information and vowed to have dinner every Sunday at his mother's house to honor Bobby."

"Wow that is so cool. Too bad though that it took them losing him in order for them to appreciate you." Alvin said.

"I thought about that, but then again I'm just glad that they actually finally accepted me at all. You don't know how hard it was to see Bobby have to choose who he should spend his time with around the holidays. Sometimes I just sit back and start to think that things happen for a reason."

"You know what, just this morning a close friend of mind said the same exact thing. I'm more like a *whatever we do in life there will always be consequences* type of guy. Good or bad, every action causes a reaction." Alvin said

Judy replied "I don't think Bobby did anything but try to protect me that night. He certainly didn't deserve to die. If it really was like that Alvin, then everyone would be pointing a finger at someone when things go bad for them. Sometimes, like I said, you can't question everything bad that happens in life. Sometimes it's just supposed to be that way. I had to learn that the hard way in order to free myself from the guilt of that night."

"I'm sorry Judy for bringing back up your pain. You are a strong woman to see what happened to him and still be able to move forward. I don't know how long it's going to take for me to get over this," said Alvin, as tears start to form into his eyes.

"I guess I can finally tell you the whole story about how I came to be in this situation. I will try and give you the short version. Alvin took a sip of his drink and took a deep breath. I first started out dating this woman named Keisha. Things were going great between us until she called me one night and told me that she just had sex with her ex."

"What? That is so grimy," Judy said while she interrupted.

"Well I broke up with her, but believe it or not we have become the best of friends. She's about to have a baby and get married very soon. So basically we are good. Later, I met Monica. I loved everything about her. In more ways than I can count, she totally completes me. One day Keisha asked me to come over and fix her computer. So I went over there fixed it and left. Absolutely nothing happened."

Judy interrupted Alvin again and said, "Absolutely nothing happened, huh? So there was no hugging or kissing?"

"Okay I gave her a hug and kiss while I was leaving. Something like the one I gave you that day at the funeral."

Judy said, "Okay I understand."

Alvin continued, "I'm glad you understand because I told Monica where I was at that day and she totally flipped. Of course she asked me the same questions that you just did and I told her the exact same thing that I told you. Well she wasn't having it, and she broke it off with me because she didn't think I was to be trusted."

Judy looked at Alvin and said, "Wow, God bless her soul. But it sounds to me that she was already having some issues that she was trying to deal with."

"Yes, most of the people she cared about all throughout her life had either died or left her. So she was kind of on the edge about people leaving her. I guess she wanted to push me aside before I did that to her. But you have to realize. I already knew what I wanted and I tried my best to convince her of that. Anyway, one night the guys from the office and I went to this strip club just to unwind. When I got there I met this stripper name April. We drank, ended up at my place and then drank some more. I was so torn up that I didn't care about protection or anything."

Judy interrupted again and said, "Damn Alvin, you meet a girl at a strip club and had unprotected sex with her? That's not only nasty, but scary as well. I hope you didn't catch anything from her?"

"No, I didn't catch anything from her, but I gave her something. She ended up becoming pregnant," said, Alvin, bracing for Judy's response.

"Wait a minute - before you continue any more of this story, I need to take another drink. No, I think I need a double."

Judy took a couple of shots and said, "Okay Alvin, let me get this straight, you had unprotected sex with a stripper one time. She ended up pregnant and all of a sudden this baby out of nowhere just so happens to be yours? I think we better tell the bartender to leave the bottle because this is going to be a long night."

Alvin looked hurt, but he knew deep down the story sounded crazy when he was saying it out loud. "I thought you were supposed to be here for support, not to tear into me."

"I'm sorry you're right," said, Judy, remorsefully. "I'm not going to interrupt you anymore. Finish the story."

Alvin continued. "Anyway, I actually thought and felt the same way you did. One day I went over to her house and gave her the test myself, and it turned out that she was truly pregnant. As for whether or not the baby was mine, she swore up and down that she never had sex with anyone else around the time that she got pregnant. She didn't want to get an abortion because the doctors told her previously that she couldn't get pregnant. So this was her miracle baby.

"After all of that happened, Monica called me and said that she wanted to give me another chance. Of course I jumped at the opportunity. So we started dating again like nothing had happened. I got engaged to her and down the line she became pregnant as well. I didn't want to tell Monica about April because I didn't want to lose her again. I was going to wait until April's baby was born and have a DNA test preformed."

Judy held up her hands and said, "Before you go on I need to take another double." Judy took a couple more shots and said, "Alvin, I'm going to be so drunk after hearing this story, I hope I will be able to walk home. Go ahead, continue!"

Alvin took a deep breath and started again. "Well, as time went on, I sort of developed some feelings for April. I slept with her a couple of times and she quit her stripping job to prove to me that she was going to be a responsible mother and possible mate. I admit, during that part of my life I was very confused. I'm now about to have two kids on the way, and both of their mothers I wanted to be with. Deep down I kind of knew that if Monica found out about April it was going to be over, so I guess I started leaning more toward being with April."

Judy interrupted Alvin again and said, "I know I said I wasn't going to cut in again, but I do have to ask this question. Here is a woman that you didn't know from Adam, and she tells you that you got her pregnant. You were not sure if this child is yours or not, so you continued to throw everything away and catch feelings for her. On top of that, you used an excuse to not tell all this to the woman that you're supposed to love and want to marry. My question to you Alvin is, how could you let a woman that was swinging on a pole corrupt a very intelligent, distinguished gentleman like yourself?"

"See I knew this was a bad idea." Alvin said disappointingly. Alvin pulled out a $100 bill, placed on the counter and said that he was leaving.

Judy stood up and said, "Alvin, please don't leave. I know I probably had too much to drink. I was just telling you how I was feeling, that's all. Please babe, come back and finish the story. I won't say anything else."

Alvin looked at Judy and saw that she was wasted, "I don't know about finishing the story, but I will make sure that you make it home safely."

Judy started holding on to Alvin and said, "Yes, thank you. I'm sorry if you think that I am bad company for you right now. I didn't mean to be."

Alvin told the bartender to keep the change and he put his arms around Judy and helped her walk out of the bar. Alvin walked Judy home and asked her for her keys. Judy was able to hand them to him and he opened up her door and walked her to the bedroom.

As he placed her on her bed, Judy looked at Alvin in his eyes while he was undressing her and said, "Bobby, you always knew how to take care of me." Then she collapsed onto the bed.

Alvin finished taking off her clothes, leaving her panties and bra on. Then he covered her up with a blanket. He then sat in a chair that was next to her bed and fell asleep. As the sunlight began to creep into the bedroom windows, Judy woke up and saw Alvin sleeping in the chair. She got up and took off his shoes which kind of startled Alvin, but he was too tired to open his eyes.

She then helped him on to the bed, and she took his arms and wrapped them around her. She laid her head on top of his chest and whispered, "Thank you for making sure I made it home safely." She soon went back to sleep.

Later that morning, Alvin woke up and saw that Judy was laying on his chest with his arms wrapped around her.

Alvin said in a loud voice, "Oh no, what happened last night?"

Judy heard him and opened up her eyes. "Nothing happened Alvin. I saw you sleeping so uncomfortably on that chair, I just wanted to do something nice for you and placed you in the bed. That was my way of saying thank you for making sure I came home safe last night."

Alvin tried to shake off the sleepiness and said, "About last night, do you remember calling me Bobby?"

"Did I? I don't know, I was so drunk. That could be possible. I never had another man here before and you look so much like him. I probably was bugging out a little last night."

"No that's okay," Alvin replied. "I just thought it was a little weird that's all. Anyway I didn't have any intentions on staying here this long, so I am about to get up and leave."

Judy looked disappointed. "No Alvin, you still owe me the rest of the story. Continue telling me what happened."

"There really isn't much more to tell. April started becoming more jealous of Monica until one day she showed up at my job where Monica and I worked and started a whole bunch of shit. Monica left storming out and that was the last time I ever saw her alive."

"Wow, a triangle of love. So what are you going to do about April?" Judy asked.

"Right now I really can't stand that bitch. If she didn't come to my job, Monica would have been alive today."

"Okay I see you pointing that finger again," said, Judy. "Maybe if she had found another way, the results probably would have been the same. You don't know what could have happened differently. I think you should just go ahead, forgive April, and try to focus on the kid that she is carrying. But if I were you, I would still go on ahead and get that DNA test done ASAP."

Alvin nodded and said, "I understand what you are saying, but that isn't my way of thinking right now."

Alvin put on his shoes and walked to the door. Judy followed behind him and said, "Thank you for sharing yourself and your story with me Alvin. I really hope that things work out for you. I also want you to know I would be more than happy to go with you to Monica's Homecoming if you would like me to."

"I really appreciate you coming out last night and letting me get some stuff off of my chest," said, Alvin. "I'm going to go home and try to figure out what I have to do next. I also would love it if you were there for me on that day."

"Great, just let me know when and I will be there." Judy hugged Alvin and gave him a kiss on the cheek.

Alvin left and went home. Later that day, detective Jones called Alvin and told him that they were going to release Monica's body to him. Alvin agreed and started preparing for Monica's funeral. A couple of days passed. One morning Alvin's doorbell rang. When he went to answer it, he saw that it was April.

Alvin opened the door and said in a very nasty tone, "What the fuck are you doing here?"

April replied, "I know that you are mad at me Alvin. I've been crying every day since I heard the news. I am here to ask for your forgiveness."

"There isn't anything you can say to me that is going to make me clear your conscience of the fucked up thing that you did that day. That is something you are going to have to deal with on your own. Now if you will excuse me I have a funeral to plan. Get the fuck away from my door, I never want to see or hear from you ever again."

April started crying and said, "Please don't punish our baby for something that I've done. In my heart I love you so much and I just want you to understand, if I could I would do anything within my power to take back that day. But it already happened, Alvin, and being mad at me and your child isn't going to bring her back. All I am asking is that you find it in your heart to at least still care and love your child if not me. That is all I'm asking for Alvin."

Alvin replied, "Again I am going to ask you to leave and never bother me. I don't want anything to do with you or your baby. I thought I made myself clear that day!"

Alvin closed the door in April's face and watched through the glass door pane as April walked away crying. Before she could take five steps, she passed out and collapsed on the sidewalk. At first Alvin just stood there watching and waiting for her to get up. After a minute or so he opened the door and walked over to her. He saw blood coming from her head and she wasn't moving.

Alvin ran back into the house to get his phone and called 911. He then laid April on her back to make sure that she was still breathing, and put pressure on her forehead where it was bleeding until the ambulance arrived. Once EMS arrived, they worked on her until she was conscious. They asked if he was her husband and the father of the baby, and if could he ride with her to the hospital.

Alvin asked, "What's wrong with her?"

The EMS tech said, "It looks like when she fell she hit her head on the concrete, it gave her a concussion and she passed out. There could be some other problems that we are unaware of, so our main concern right now is getting her to the hospital to make sure that she and the baby are okay."

"I will come to the hospital, but will it be okay if I just followed you in my car? That way we will be able to get back home when the time comes."

The EMS tech said "Sure, no problem. If you are ready just follow us."

Alvin hopped in his car and followed the ambulance to the hospital. Once there, they took April to an isolated room in the emergency ward. They asked Alvin to wait by the Administration office to fill out some paper work. A couple of hours passed by and a doctor named Wilson came out to let Alvin know what's going on with April.

Dr. Wilson said, "Hello My name is Dr. Wilson. Are you April Alston's husband?"

Alvin shook his head no and said, "But I am the father of her baby. How are they?"

Dr. Wilson said, "Do you know of anyone who might be able to make decisions for her in the case that she wouldn't be able to make them for herself?"

Alvin, getting a little nervous and upset said, "Could you please tell me what happened?"

Dr. Wilson replied, "As far as the baby is concerned she's very healthy. I don't see any problem with her what so ever. Her mother on the other hand is awake, but she appears to be in a somewhat vegetative state. We did a CAT scan and MRI and we found a tremendous amount of damage on the left side of her brain, probably caused when she hit her head on the ground."

"There is still a large amount of blood in there, so we are just going to have to see once we remove some of it. After that, the best we can do is to monitor her to see if she will improve. I don't really want to alarm you, but in most of these cases that we have like this, it usually turns for the worst."

"But what happens if she never recovers? What will happen to the baby?" said, Alvin, visibly upset now.

"To decide that sir, we would have to sit down and talk about all of the options. Unfortunately, since you are not her husband, I really need to speak to a family member so that I would know what to do next."

"As far as I know she was an only child and both of her parents are deceased. When it comes to family I am all that she has."

Dr. Wilson said, "I understand what you are saying sir, but it's company policy to wait at least 48 hours before we can even consider you. But if her condition takes a dramatic turn within the next 24 hours then I would have no choice but to let you take responsibility for her."

Alvin reached out to shake the doctor's hands and thanked him. While Alvin sat in the waiting room, he thought about all the things that were happening to him. He folded his hands in front of his face and said a quiet prayer to himself. Soon after, Dr. Wilson walked in and asked to speak to him in the lobby.

Dr. Wilson said, "I have great news. We were able to relieve the pressure on her brain by removing the excess blood and stopping the bleeding. As far as I can see she should be alright. She has been responding by moving one of her fingers whenever I ask her a question. So that's a good sign that she is responsive enough to know what's going on and no longer at risk of becoming brain dead."

Alvin looked up toward the ceiling and said, "Thank you God."

He then asked if he could go see her, but Dr. Wilson said, "I think we are going to let her rest a little while longer before she can see you. We have to try our best to keep her clam for at least a few hours."

"I understand. I actually have to prepare a funeral for someone that I really care for."

"I am so sorry to hear that. I hope that things go well for you and I will have you in my prayers." Replied Dr. Wilson.

"Thank you, I could use all the help I can get."

Alvin left the hospital and went to B. Lane funeral home to pay for Monica's homecoming. Once there he spared no expense making sure that Monica had the best homecoming he has ever seen. He started to head back to the hospital to check up on April, but he decided to go home and rest awhile.

With so much on his mind, as soon and he arrived home he picked up the phone and gave Keisha a call. "Alvin! I was just thinking about you. Are you alright?"

"Yes, I just came back from the funeral home. I picked out a nice casket and beautiful white roses for her and the baby. Everything is going to take place this Friday."

"Alvin that sounds really nice. You know I will be there for you. Just text me all of the information."

"You are about to pop in a few months. It will be okay if you can't make it. Besides, I know you will be getting married soon and need to plan out your future for both your husband and baby."

"No, I will be okay Alvin. Right now being there for you is way too important for me,"

"Alright, I really appreciate the support. Unfortunately, I do have more bad news to tell you."

Keisha replied, "Oh Alvin please! I can't with you and this bad news stuff, you're killing me! Alvin was shock to hear her response.

"Trust me I know how you feel. But it's okay, I will fill you in some other time."

"No, tell me now. I'm sorry for being so insensitive. What happened?" said, Keisha, on the edge of her seat.

"Well April came by my house trying to apologize."

Keisha immediately cut Alvin off and said, "That trick! What in the hell did she want? Do she honestly think that you would have anything to do with her knowing what she did?"

Alvin said, "Keisha if you clam down I can tell you the rest of the story, then you can get all mad afterward."

"Yes sorry about that Alvin," Keisha replied. "But she worked on my last nerve when you first told me about her. Go ahead baby, I am sorry."

Alvin continued, "Well we kind of got into it and I slammed my door in her face."

Keisha chuckled and said, "That's good for that bitch. I hope you don't mess with her any more Alvin. Do what you have to do to take care of your kid if you find out that it's yours after the DNA test, but please leave her ass right where she need to be. Riding up and down on somebody pole!"

"Keisha you are making this very difficult for me right now. When she was walking down my walkway she fell and hit her head on the ground."

Keisha gasped and said, "Knowing her it was probably a trick to see if you would come running to her side."

"No she was actually unconscious and I had to call EMS to come get her."

Keisha said "As much as I hate her right now I can't say that I would wish for anything that bad to happen to her. How's the baby?"

"The baby is fine. For a moment there it looked as though she was about to go into a vegetative state. The doctor was able to drain some blood out of her brain which prevented that from happening. Right now both her and the baby are in stable condition."

"Damn Alvin, I don't know if I should take that as bad news or good news. You have me all twisted up right now. But like I said, I wouldn't wish for anything bad to happen to her. The best thing you can do is put it in God's hands and pray that everything is going to be alright."

"Yes I already have," Alvin replied. "Right now that's the only thing that is keeping me going."

Alvin and Keisha talked for a couple of more hours and then hung up. The next day Alvin went to the hospital to check up on April. As soon as he walked into the room he noticed all the machines that she was hooked up to. Just as he was about to walk to her bedside, April's eyes opened wide. Tears started flowing down her face and she was able to motion her fingers as to say come closer.

Alvin walked closer to her side and April started shuddering, "Than Than Thank u Al Al Al Alvin for for for Ssss Sssss sav saving us."

Alvin Put one hand on top of April's hand and the other toward his lips and said, "Shhhh, Don't talk. Just listen. Monica meant the world to me, and it was you who took her away from me. When we first got together, I just knew that she was the woman of my dreams. Nothing hurt me more in the world than that first time she walked away from me. I would have done anything to get her back. So much so, that when I saw you and saw how much you looked like her, I couldn't resist being with you just to fantasize that I was being with her.

That baby, that baby that she was carrying, that was going to be my first born son. You also took that away from me. Now out of all this craziness, somehow or another I loved you just enough to even consider leaving her to be with you. How fucked up is that? Forgive me for saying this, but as much as I may still have some kind of deep dark feelings for you, right now I don't give a damn about you.

Here is what is going to happen. When my daughter is born you will sign her over to me and I will raise her as a single father. You will stay out our lives until I feel you have suffered as much as I am suffering now. Fight me if you want on this, but I guarantee I will make your life a living hell every step of the way. Hell would be a vacation by the time I get finished with you. If you understand and agree with what I am saying just nod your head."

April did not move. Then with a devilish smile on her face she replied, "I I I I Wil Wil Always lov lov u Alvin and we we will be 2 ge gether. Bbbelieve that!"

Alvin removed his hand away from her with disgust. "You are fucking crazy! I'm totally convinced now that I have to stay as far away from you that I can."

Alvin turned away and walked out of the room.

During the day of Monica's homecoming, the church where it was held was packed. Alvin had white roses everywhere. In the front laid a white coffins trimmed with gold. He thought about having the baby removed from Monica and have her hold him in her arms, but he then decided to just keep them as one.

Judy and Keisha sat next to Alvin the entire time. When it became time for Alvin to give her eulogy, he hesitated before going up.

Once Alvin was up standing in front of everyone, in a crackling voice he said, "I would like to thank everyone here for coming out to see my beautiful Monica who is carrying my son whom I named Junior, off to be with God. This is going to be tough for me because of how much she really meant to me. So please be patient with me.

"Monica was in every sense of the word an Angel on earth. Sometimes people go through things in life that feels unfair. My Monica took life with all of the good and bad things and made a good life for herself. Everyone here who knew her, knows that she would do anything to make sure you had a good day. She was one of the most unselfish person I know. She hardly asks for anything, but she gave a whole lot of herself and anything she had to make sure the people around her were happy.

"I am so happy that I had the chance to get to spend my life with her during her last days. I would like to leave all of you with this one important note. No matter how hard life is, try to find someone, anyone to talk to. Hurting someone dear to you because you are hurting isn't the answer. Because to live another day, gives you another chance to do things over.

"It will give that person you love, another chance to say *I'm sorry*. It will give your children an opportunity to live and learn from your mistakes. Nothing is more precious than to wake up in the morning and have another chance at life, to erase all the wrong from the day before. May God keep my baby and my love forever close by his side."

Alvin stepped down, stood in front of Monica's body and started to cry. Judy immediately got up and started hugging Alvin, saying it's going to be alright. After everything was over, Alvin asked Judy if it would be okay if he could come over to her place.

Judy was so overwhelmed with delight that Alvin had ask her that question. "You know I would love to have you over Alvin. Anytime you wish you can just come over and we can talk." Alvin gave her a big hug and kissed her on the forehead.

Many years had passed since that day. Judy and Alvin got married and had a two-year-old son named; Alvin the third.

When April had her daughter; She named her Alicia. Alvin had her tested and found out that she was indeed his daughter.

It didn't take long for Alvin to forgive April for the death of Monica. He loved his daughter so much, he tried to spend as much time with her as possible.

Once April knew that she didn't have a chance to be with Alvin, she tried her best to stay out of his relationship with Judy. Eventually she saved up enough money to open up a beauty shop of her own.

She met a nice guy name Earl, and they soon wed and had another daughter name Emily. Every chance she got, she would always thank Alvin for walking into the club that night and saving her life. Their relationship remained respectful and they both learned to have great admiration for one another.

Keisha was married and had a daughter name Kasandra. It didn't take long for her to get pregnant again and she had a son name Lenny. Both she and Alvin remain the best friends and was always there for one another. Through the good times, and bad times.

Looking back at the beginning of his journey, Alvin realized that he had accomplished what he set out to do after all - to have, a loving family!

THE END

www.ingramcontent.com/pod-product-compliance
Lightning Source LLC
Chambersburg PA
CBHW051253170626
46809CB00004B/1623